NANCY DREW® AND THE HARDY BOYS®
SUPER SLEUTHS!

NANCY DREW® AND THE HARDY BOYS®

SUPER SLEUTHS!

Seven New Mysteries

by Carolyn Keene and Franklin W. Dixon

Illustrated by Paul Frame

W Wanderer Books
Published by Simon and Schuster, New York

Copyright © 1981 by Stratemeyer Syndicate
Published by WANDERER BOOKS
A Simon & Schuster Division of
Gulf & Western Corporation
Simon & Schuster Building
1230 Avenue of the Americas
New York, New York 10020

Manufactured in the United States of America
10 9 8 7 6 5 4 3 2 1
NANCY DREW and THE HARDY BOYS are
trademarks of Stratemeyer Syndicate,
registered in the United States Patent and
Trademark Office
WANDERER and colophon are trademarks of
Simon & Schuster

"The Secret of Mountaintop Inn" was first
published in *Family Circle* magazine on
December 16, 1980 as "Solve a Christmas Mystery."

Library of Congress Cataloging in Publication Data

Keene, Carolyn.
    Nancy Drew and the Hardy boys, super
sleuths!

    "Wanderer books."
    Contents: The bank robbery puzzle—Clue in
the chimes—The interlocking maze—[etc.]
    1. Detective and mystery stories, American.   2.
Children's stories, American.   [1. Mystery and
detective stories.   2. Short stories] I. Dixon,
Franklin W. II. Frame, Paul, ill.   III.
Title.
PZ7.K23Nae   [Fic]   81-14496
ISBN 0-671-44429-8   AACR2
ISBN 0-671-43375-X (pbk.)

contents

foreword

Dear Fans,
When we were asked to write a book of short stories in which Nancy Drew and the Hardy Boys solve mysteries, we found this a real challenge. We felt that Nancy should not grab the limelight, or Hardy readers would disapprove. If the boys stole the show, girl readers would think this very unfair. What to do? We finally decided to give these three characters equal time and let the plots develop into a collection of exciting mysteries filled with fun and wholesome adventure. We hope you enjoy them. Let us know.

C. K. and F. W. D.

MISTAKEN IDENTITY

"**A**nother package for you, Joe," Mrs. Hardy called out from the foot of the stairs.

Her younger son, a healthy-looking blond seventeen-year-old, hurried down the steps. "Is there a sender's name and address?" he asked.

"No," his slim, attractive mother replied. "It's just like the other packages."

Recently, Joe had been receiving mysterious gifts through the mail, including pieces of valuable jewelry and several hundred dollars in cash. But there was no clue to the identity of the sender!

"This is weird," Joe said as he opened the box. His eyes bulged and he gasped. "A diamond necklace! Why would anybody send such a thing to me?"

"If you don't want it, give it to Nancy Drew," replied his dark-haired brother Frank, who was a year older, as he appeared in the hallway. "She's coming today for a visit, you know."

"That's right," Joe said, looking at his wrist-watch, "and it's time for us to head for the airport to meet her."

The boys waved good-bye to their mother and to their Aunt Gertrude, who was busy preparing lunch, and then drove off in their sports sedan to the Bayport airfield. Nancy's plane had just arrived. Frank and Joe greeted the attractive, reddish-blond-haired girl, then the three went to the baggage-claim area.

Joe's eyes twinkled. "Miss Famous Girl Detective," he said, "you've come in the nick of time to help solve a mystery."

"Wonderful." Nancy smiled, then added quickly, "What's it about?"

"Joe has a secret admirer," Frank replied. "She sends him diamond necklaces, rings, and—"

"Aw, cut it out," Joe said, as he picked up Nancy's bag. Together, the trio walked to the boys' yellow car. To keep his brother from further kidding, Joe told Nancy the story of the mysterious packages.

"And there's no clue to the sender on any of them?" she asked as Frank drove off.

"No, they've all been sent from different towns addressed to me, care of General Delivery, Bayport."

"You mean," Nancy said, "the packages were from different locations?"

"That's right," Frank replied. "It's strange. Apparently, the sender didn't want to go to the same post office twice."

"Or," said Joe, "he's moving fast from place to place. We suspect the money and jewelry might have been stolen, so we notified the police. Chief Collig is holding the money but suggested we keep the jewelry in Dad's safe, and try to solve the mystery. We got a call today from Dave Jones, the postmaster. He wants to see us. I hope he can tell us something about this."

Nancy was silent for a minute, then asked if Joe had examined the wrappings of the gifts.

"Yes," he said, "but there was no writing on them. However, we can look again. I'm sure Aunt Gertrude has saved the papers. She never throws anything away."

When Nancy and the boys reached the Hardys' large old-fashioned house, Nancy hurried inside and was hugged by Mrs. Hardy, then by Aunt Gertrude, Mr. Hardy's sister who had lived with them for some time. She was apt to be a bit strict, but the boys took her scoldings and peppery advice good-naturedly.

"I certainly hope, Nancy, that you can catch

the crazy person who's sending things to Joe. These boys have been flitting here and there without finding a clue!"

Frank and Joe colored with embarrassment.

Nancy laughed. "Maybe the case needs a woman's touch! Aunt Gertrude, did you save the wrappers, tissues, boxes—whatever the mystery articles came in?"

"Indeed I did," she replied. "I'll get them."

She went to a closet in the kitchen. "Thank goodness for these old houses with plenty of storage space," she remarked. "Here's everything. I kept it all together." Aunt Gertrude lifted out a tall trash basket and set it near the kitchen table. Each wrapping paper had been carefully folded.

Nancy took one, opened it, and painstakingly scanned both sides. From her handbag, she removed a strong magnifying glass she always carried with her. Meanwhile, the others had started to examine the boxes.

Suddenly, Nancy said, "Here's something. A name has been covered by black ink, but I can still read it, I think. It says—" She held the magnifier closer to the marks. "It says KERMIT & SONS. Does that ring a bell in your minds?"

Mrs. Hardy spoke up. "I believe that's a

jewelry store in Congdon about fifty miles from here."

Aunt Gertrude smirked at her nephews. "I told you Nancy Drew would find a clue."

Frank and Joe laughed at the jibe, and Frank asked, "Joe, do you recall what came in this paper?"

His brother examined the creases. "I believe a small box did."

He hurried to the safe and soon returned with a plain white box. Inside, on layers of cotton, lay a gold bracelet studded with small diamonds!

"It's gorgeous!" Nancy exclaimed.

The three detectives discussed how they should proceed with the clue. Frank suggested, "Why don't we drive over to Congdon and quiz Kermit & Sons? Then on the way back, we can stop at the post office."

"Good idea," Joe agreed. "How about it, Nancy?"

"Okay."

Aunt Gertrude said, "Don't take the bracelet with you. You might be robbed!"

"If we don't show the bracelet, how can it be identified?" Joe asked.

"He's right," Nancy said. "I'll wear it. That

way it'll be safer. With you two fellows guarding me, I certainly can't come to any harm."

Upon reaching the Congdon store, the three went inside. Nancy walked up to a salesman and said, "I wonder if you can help solve a mystery for me."

She took off the bracelet and laid it on the counter. "This was sent without an enclosure card or a return address. But I deduced from the wrapping that it was purchased here. Can you confirm this?"

The man picked up the bracelet and studied it. "I'm not sure," he said. "Let me show it to Mr. Kermit."

He was gone about five minutes, then returned with a somber-looking, gray-haired man.

"I'm Mr. Kermit," he introduced himself. "This bracelet did, indeed, come from my shop. But it was not purchased. It was stolen!"

Nancy and the Hardys exchanged glances. Just as they had suspected, Joe had received stolen property!

"Who are you?" the jeweler inquired.

The young people introduced themselves and showed their driver's licenses.

"Fenton Hardy's sons?" Mr. Kermit asked in surprise. "I know your dad." He chuckled. "Detective Hardy would have the laugh on me if he knew I suspected you three might be up to something illegal!"

Joe explained about the mysterious packages he had been receiving. Mr. Kermit said, "I'll get my catalog and prove to you that the bracelet is mine."

Nancy asked, "If you've had other jewelry stolen, may we see the list? Joe may have received some of it."

Mr. Kermit disappeared for a few moments, then returned with a printed brochure and a sheet taken from an accounting ledger. "Here's a picture and a description of the bracelet," he said, indicating an illustration.

Nancy looked at it intently, then read the printed matter beneath. "This certainly describes the piece," she agreed.

Meanwhile, the boys were studying the handwritten notation on the ledger sheet. "That clinches the theft of the bracelet," Joe said. "Are there any others?"

The jeweler took another paper from his pocket and read off the list of stolen articles. Several of them, like the bracelet, had been taken over a year before. None of them, however, had been sent to Joe.

Frank suggested, "Mr. Kermit, why don't we ask the police in Bayport, where we're from, to hold the bracelet until the mystery is solved? Chief Collig is already safeguarding cash that was mailed to Joe."

The jeweler did not reply. He was looking beyond the young detectives at two policemen who had just entered his shop.

"Are these the people who turned up with your stolen property?" one of the officers asked.

Mr. Kermit replied, "I think we've straightened everything out. Sorry to have bothered you." After admitting to the young people that he had called headquarters when he first saw the bracelet, he introduced them to the policemen.

"What!" the second officer exclaimed. "You've caught Joe Hardy but don't want him arrested?"

"No. He's done nothing wrong!"

The officer pulled a memo sheet from a pocket, unfolded it, and held up a police notice. "Read this and then tell me he's done nothing wrong!"

The whole group looked at it and gasped. The notice read:

UNKNOWN THIEF WANTED IN SEVERAL STATES.
NO DESCRIPTION OR ADDRESS AVAILABLE.
USES MANY ALIASES.

A list was given. At the bottom was the name:
JOE HARDY!

"Wow!" Joe cried out. "A thief is using my name!"

Mr. Kermit spoke up. "I've already checked with the chief in Bayport where this Joe Hardy comes from."

Frank burst out, "My brother is no thief!"

Nancy added, "And I can attest to that."

Joe then explained his strange predicament to the officers. When they realized that Joe was telling the truth and that the young sleuths were also investigating the crime, the men were apologetic. One said with a wry smile, "I guess we'd better match wits with these three amateur detectives or they'll beat us solving the mystery."

They all laughed, then Nancy, Frank, and Joe excused themselves and said good-bye. They drove directly to the post office back in Bayport, hoping to receive some helpful information there. When they arrived, they went to the postmaster's office to speak with Mr. Jones.

"Hi there, boys," Dave Jones greeted them. "And who's your pretty friend?"

"Hi, Mr. Jones. This is Nancy Drew. She's visiting from River Heights," Frank said.

Nancy smiled and shook the postmaster's

hand. "Pleased to meet you. Actually, Mr. Jones, I'm here to help Frank and Joe solve a mystery. Maybe you can help us."

"Well, I do have something interesting to tell you. Yesterday afternoon, a man came in here, said he was Joe Hardy, and asked me to give him his mail! I told him that I knew Joe Hardy personally and he certainly wasn't the Joe Hardy I knew. He looked mighty surprised and hightailed it out of here. I haven't seen him since, but I thought you should know. Does that have anything to do with the mystery you're working on?"

"I'm not sure, but you're right, it is interesting. What did this man look like?" Joe asked. The postmaster told him the man had a scraggly beard and short brown hair, and was about six feet tall.

"As I said, he hightailed it out of here pretty fast. I didn't get a very good look at him."

"Thanks a lot, Mr. Jones. You've been a great help. If you should see him again, call either me or the police. We'll let Chief Collig know."

The three young detectives then headed for home, discussing the day's incidents. They were greeted at the door by Aunt Gertrude, who was amazed at their story. "Ridiculous! Utterly ridiculous!" she sputtered after hearing what had happened. "First Joe being accused of commiting crimes which probably were done by a man twice his age. Probably a hardened criminal. And then to have someone posing as Joe to pick up his mail!"

Mrs. Hardy came forward, sympathized with her son, then handed him a package. "Here's another one for you, Joe. Again, no sender's name or address."

Joe unwrapped the package, being careful not to destroy any clue it might hold, including fingerprints. Inside, carefully enclosed in a Styrofoam mold, lay the beautiful silver figurine of a man riding horseback. The piece had been intricately fashioned. The rider's features and hands, the stirrups, and the animal's nostrils had been delicately made.

"This figurine must be very valuable," Nancy said, picking up the wrapping to examine it.

"Priceless," Aunt Gertrude remarked. "It's quite beautiful. Well, you young folks must be starved. Dinner is ready to be put on the table."

Frank begged for a few minutes to inspect the horseman. He asked to borrow Nancy's magnifying glass, and reported that, as far as he could tell, there were no fingerprints on the piece. He looked intently at a mark on the bottom of one hoof.

"Here's something!" he exclaimed. "A hall-mark. Looks like the imprint of a horseshoe."

"Tomorrow morning," Nancy said, "let's phone Chief Collig to find out if he has a record of any stolen property which includes this horse and rider."

She did so and learned that the figurine had been stolen from the Lakeville museum about a year before. The thief had never been caught.

"Bring the horseman down here," the chief advised. "I'll have people from the Lakeville Museum come over to identify it. I understand the piece is the only one of its kind and is very old and valuable."

On the way to deliver it, Frank said to Joe and Nancy, "One thing puzzles me. If the thief was operating in this area, why don't the police know anything about him?"

Nancy reminded him that the figurine had been stolen a year before. "The thief could have gone many states away in the meantime and could be back now. Incidentally, have you checked with the post office today? Has anyone been back?"

"Yes, I did check," Joe replied. "No one's been back—at least not as Joe Hardy!"

When the group reached headquarters, Chief Collig greeted Nancy, both hands outstretched.

"With you joining the Hardys in solving this case, the villain doesn't stand a chance."

Nancy laughed and blushed slightly, then said, "With such belief in me, I don't dare fail!"

The chief was intrigued by the figurine the young people showed him. He said that whoever sent it had polished the silver piece so any tarnish or fingerprints were gone completely.

This remark gave Nancy an idea. She asked, "Do you think the thief or a pal of his works in a place that repairs or restores unusual jewelry and artifacts?"

"Could be," Chief Collig agreed. "I'll check on that."

He called in a sergeant and requested him to look in the files for such a person. Before he returned, Mr. Tompkin, a representative from the museum, arrived and was mystified by Joe's story.

"This is the horseman taken from our collection of very fine figurines," Mr. Tompkin said. "The horseshoe hallmark is old and every piece bearing it is one of a kind. Most of the figurines were made to order."

Arrangements were made for the museum to retrieve the piece, and the man left. As the three young people were about to go, the sergeant returned.

"I think I have an answer to your question, Chief. A man named Alex Wyzucker, who was an expert jewelry repair worker for a big exclusive firm in town, went to prison for absconding with money from the company."

"Where is he now?" Nancy asked.

"No one knows. After he was released, he disappeared."

Joe spoke up. "Sounds as if he could be a real suspect in our case."

"Did you get a description of him?" Nancy inquired.

"Yes. Five feet five. Straight black hair that is parted on the left side. Very white skin. Sharp features. Wears glasses. Thin. Forty years old."

"Was he ever known to be a jewel thief?" Nancy asked.

"He was never convicted on that charge," the sergeant replied.

Since there was nothing more the three young detectives could do, they promised to keep working on the case, then drove off.

That evening they told the whole story to the family. Mr. Hardy, tall, straight, keen-eyed, congratulated the trio on their progress.

"I wish we had a picture of this Alex Wyzucker," he said.

Nancy spoke up. "I'll try to draw a likeness of

him from the police description," and went to get her sketching pad and charcoal pencils. As soon as dinner was over, she sat down to work.

Within an hour, she had made three drawings of a short, thin man with black hair parted on the left side. He had sharp features and was wearing glasses. There were front, side, and back views, which Frank taped to the edge of the mantel above the fireplace in the living room.

A smile spread over Mr. Hardy's face. "The sketches certainly follow the description. Excellent work, Nancy. Now find your man!"

"We'll start first thing tomorrow," Frank said.

Everybody slept soundly until shortly after one o'clock, when they were all awakened by a shrieking siren. It was the burglar alarm system in the house.

Someone was trying to break in!

Within seconds, every member of the Hardy family and Nancy were in the second-floor hall, gazing at a position board which showed where the intruder was: at one of the dining room windows! Mr. Hardy immediately turned on a master switch which was connected with every light in the house. Then he started down the stairs, the others following.

Suddenly, Nancy had an idea. She ran back to

her bedroom, which was above the dining room, and stared out the window. If the intruder had become scared and run away, she reasoned, he would be speeding across the lawn to the street.

She saw no one but heard a car motor running. Was a confederate waiting for the burglar? On a hunch, she quickly slipped into sport shoes and street clothes, then grabbed her coat from the closet.

As Nancy hurried to the first floor, two steps at a time, she heard Mr. Hardy say, "I guess that burglar didn't get in."

"Thank goodness!" Aunt Gertrude exclaimed.

"I'm not so sure," Nancy spoke up quickly. "My sketches are gone! Did any of you take them?"

"No," the others chorused, and Mrs. Hardy said fearfully, "The thief may still be in the house."

Nancy whispered to Frank and Joe, "Grab your jackets and let's look outside." As they pulled their jackets from the hall closet, she said, "Follow me! I heard a car motor running on the side street. It's still there!"

"I'll get our car," Frank said and dashed off.

Nancy and Joe vaulted the hedge and ran out

to the street. The waiting vehicle was a panel truck, its rear doors open. A small man was running toward it. He climbed inside and pulled the doors shut.

Joe and Nancy memorized the license plate as they dashed after the truck. They had gone only to the next intersection, where the fugitive driver had turned, when Frank caught up to them in the yellow sports sedan. They hopped in beside him and he took off after the speeding truck.

"Wow!" Frank said. "Those guys are breaking the law by about twenty miles an hour!"

Meanwhile, Joe had picked up their short-wave radio and located the police band. The officer on duty was surprised at the message.

"Let me write this down. You're chasing a panel truck—repeat that license number—I have it—I'll notify the state police at once and your family. Keep me informed."

The pursuit went on for many miles, with Joe reporting their location every few minutes. Finally, the truck turned off the main road onto a lane full of potholes and large, loose stones. Frank slowed down, afraid of breaking the car's springs or ruining the tires. Soon he lost track of the truck.

Joe groaned. "This is all we need! Tell you

what. Nancy, you take the wheel. Frank and I can run faster through the fields alongside the road than we can drive."

"Good idea," Frank agreed.

He stopped the car and jumped out. Nancy slid over to the driver's seat. The two boys took off at top speed and managed to outdistance Nancy, who did not dare go over ten miles an hour. Stones pelted the undercarriage of the sports sedan and she had to hold the wheel firmly to keep on a straight course. The boys were soon out of sight. Nancy realized she was alone in unknown territory and an eerie feeling came over her.

Suddenly, the car's telephone buzzed and she jumped. Regaining her composure, she picked up the mike. "Hello. Who is this?"

"Who are *you?*" a man's voice asked sternly.

"A friend of the owners of this car," she replied.

The man chuckled. "This is police headquarters. You must be Nancy Drew. Where are Frank and Joe?"

"Just ahead of me."

The officer went on, "The state police are trying to find them. Where are you?"

"On the same road Joe last told you about. It's full of stones and potholes."

"Okay. Be careful and keep me informed."

"Oh!" Nancy exclaimed. The mike nearly dropped from her hand but she managed to put it down, as the car came to an abrupt halt. The right front wheel was wedged in a deep hole! Nancy climbed out and examined it. The tire seemed to be all right, but could she free the wheel? After a few minutes, the determined girl decided to try backing up the car.

As she was about to put it into reverse gear, the girl detective became aware of headlights behind her. Turning, she was relieved to see revolving blue lights atop an approaching car.

"The police!" Nancy sighed in relief.

Meanwhile, Frank and Joe had spotted the panel truck, which pulled up to a deserted, ramshackle farmhouse. Two men got out, stumbled through the darkness to a door, and went inside. A third man with a lantern led them into a large room. He stood the light on a crate and the three sat down on the floor.

Frank whispered in Joe's ear, "That small one looks like Nancy's sketches! He must be—"

At this moment, the man who had carried the light demanded, "Okay, Wyzucker, hand over my stuff!"

"I ain't got it!"

"What!"

Wyzucker turned to the truck driver. "Spanner, you tell him."

"We did just what you told Wy to do. I rented a panel truck, waited on the side street, and left the engine running. Alex here sneaked up to the house at one o'clock. It was dark. Everybody was asleep."

As he paused, the would-be burglar continued, "I used the jimmy you gave me, Chick, and only opened the dining room window a crack to see if an alarm would go off. It didn't. Then I went to the living room window and flashed my light inside. Hanging from the mantel were three sketches of me! I guess that somehow the police must have given them to the Hardys."

Frank and Joe smiled. How wrong he was! Just then, they heard footsteps behind them and realized Nancy and four policemen had joined them.

Wyzucker went on with his story. "I knew then Joe Hardy was after me. My first thought was to get the pictures back."

"That was dumb!" snarled Chick. "Then what?"

"I guess I panicked. Suddenly the burglar alarm siren went off—delayed action from that window I jimmied. I broke the front window, crawled in, and tore off the sketches. They're in my pocket. I'll show 'em to you!"

"You idiot!" Chick groaned. "Then you ran?"

"Not right away. Suddenly all the house lights went on. I tried to hide. There was no place, so I went out the window and to the truck. No chance to get your stolen stuff."

"You're not only a fool, Wyzucker, but the dumbest one I ever met."

"Whadda ya mean? I told you I was never a burglar. And you're the dumb one with that crazy idea of having me dig up your loot and send it to you as Joe Hardy, care of General Delivery, Bayport.

"But you never notified me to tell me you had mailed them. I wasn't expecting anything for some time. Then when you told me you'd been sending them all along, I went to the post office. They told me that the packages had been delivered to Joe Hardy! I could've died! Listen, Wyzucker, you get those 'gifts' back, or your life won't be worth a plugged nickel!"

When there was no answer, Chick got up and went over to Alex. He yanked him to his feet and slapped him so hard on one cheek that the small man rocked on his heels.

Outside, Police Officer Roberts, who had joined the three detectives, whispered to his group, "I think it's time for us to move in!"

On tiptoe, the young people followed him to the door and inside to the big room. Before the three crooks could draw concealed weapons, the police strong-armed them, then asked Joe if he would like to slip a pair of handcuffs on the thief who had borrowed the name Joe Hardy and jeopardized the boy's reputation so the Congdon police had nearly arrested him as a thief.

Joe grinned. "There's nothing I'd rather do," he said, locking the steel bracelets around the man's wrists. "By the way, Chick, what's your real name?"

Officer Roberts answered for him. "We've just learned it's Grimes Chiklaw. He and Wyzucker met in prison. Wy was released, but Chiklaw was to serve another five years for attempted robbery. He escaped and was afraid to be spotted until he could grow a beard and dye his hair. He holed up in different places. Wy, meanwhile, was to collect stolen items that Chiklaw had hidden in various places and mail them to Chiklaw. Some had been buried and were in bad shape, so Wy had polished them.

Wyzucker suddenly decided to talk. "When

he found the goods were sent to a real Joe Hardy by mistake, he ordered me to get them back or else. So I tried tonight but failed." The beaten man hung his head.

Nancy asked, "Who is the truck driver?"

Officer Roberts surprised everyone by replying, "He's one of our men—Charlie. You can take off those fake handcuffs. Charlie managed to find Wy and make friends with him by pretending he had been a getaway driver for a crook."

Charlie said, "But I didn't learn where Chiklaw was staying until we reached here. I'd have felt a lot better had I known Nancy Drew and the Hardys were following us with the police! I couldn't have arrested those two by myself. Thanks for your help, you guys."

Frank grinned. "Now all we have to do is to track down the owners of the other stolen goods."

Nancy had a hunch. "How about searching Chicklaw and his luggage? Maybe he has some record of his former activities in there."

No list was found by the police on the thief or in his luggage, but Wy decided to volunteer a clue.

"Chicklaw mentioned to me that in his spare time he wrote a tricky list—"

"Shut up!" Chicklaw screamed.

Nancy, Frank, and Joe had been searching the room.

"Here's a paper!" Frank called out, and opened a folded sheet he had pulled from a crack between floorboards. "Listen to this. Sugar, Freemont, coffee, Beason, milk—. Names inserted in a grocery list. They must be the people he robbed!"

Chiklaw would admit nothing at first, but finally burst out with an ugly, "These kids are too smart!"

It was already daylight when the police drove away with their prisoners. Nancy and the Hardys headed for home. All were weary, so there was little conversation.

Joe, however, said with a yawn, "I'm glad that fake Joe Hardy's going to prison and won't have an opportunity to use my *good name* again."

Frank could not resist a little barb. "Anyway, you're a *good sleuth.*"

Nancy smiled.

THE PIRATE COVE TREASURE

"**R**ace you to shore, Nancy!" Joe Hardy called out from his surfboard.

"Okay," said Nancy Drew, who was balancing herself on her own board.

Joe was alongside her, with his brother Frank surfing a little distance behind. There had been a slight lull in the turbulent water, but the three young people watched as a tremendous swell built. They would be caught in the curl of the wave and probably knocked into the water.

To avoid losing their boards, the three surfers dropped down and clung tightly to them. The crashing wave carried them ahead at breakneck speed. Suddenly, something rammed into Nancy and banged her arm: the board of another surfer!

The pain was so intense that Nancy lost her hold on the board and fell into the water. She felt dizzy but realized she must swim to shore or drown!

Meanwhile, Joe had outdistanced Nancy and did not know what had happened. Frank, however, had seen the accident and felt it had been caused deliberately. The stranger, an expert surfer, had ridden off, paying no attention to Nancy.

Frank, a strong swimmer, realized that Nancy could never make it to shore without assistance. Abandoning his board, he swiftly swam to her side and offered, "Let me help you."

Nancy, her injured arm getting numb, was grateful for Frank's assistance. They braved the waves, which, though strong, helped to carry them to shore where Joe was standing.

"What happened?" he asked, taking Nancy's hand and leading her out of the water.

Frank told him. "The skunk!" Joe exploded. "I saw that guy zoom up here. He hugged his surfboard and raced away as if a shark were after him."

"Did you see his face?"

"Sure did. Has black hair and a square jaw. Tough and mean-looking. I could certainly identify him. I wonder if he's connected with our case."

Frank suggested that Nancy go to her hotel room and rest. The brothers helped the injured girl into her beach robe and Frank escorted her across the sand to the hotel.

As they walked along the beach, they discussed the case that had brought them to the island of Spanish Wells. A valuable treasure chest had been found and was to be included in an exhibition that would open the island's first historical museum. Mr. Davison, the museum's owner and curator, was quite excited about the treasure chest; it was an important find and would be the center of attention. But with only a week to go before the opening, the chest had been stolen from the museum's basement. Mr. Davison, a friend of Nancy's father, had asked for help. The Hardys and the Drews joined forces to find the stolen treasure in time for the opening.

"We have only a few days left," Joe said with a sigh. "I hope we'll be able to do it. Maybe our dads will have some information when they arrive later."

When the three young people reached the hotel, Frank took Nancy to her room, while Joe went back to the beach to try to retrieve the surfboards they had left in the water after the accident. As he reached the shoreline, he could see them being tossed about in the surf.

"They belong to you?" a voice called.

Joe turned to see a figure coming toward him. A slender but muscular man with a close-cropped, scraggly white beard smiled at the boy. The elderly stranger was wearing a pirate's outfit, which included red knee breeches, a ragged, yellow silk shirt, and a rakish green bandanna with a tassel over one ear. He was barefoot and carried a lightweight metal detector.

"Yes, the surfboards are my brother's and a friend's," Joe replied, gazing curiously at the man. "What do you think are my chances of getting them back?"

"Good, unless somebody steals 'em. The boards'll come ashore, if you got patience." The man reassured him. "Me—I'm looking for my great-grandpa's treasure. He was a pirate, and a good one, mind you. He buried a treasure somewhere around here when his ship went down in the worst gale that ever hit these shores. I'll never give up huntin'—," and with this he patted his metal detector, "—until they bury *me*."

Joe asked him, "Have many treasures been found in this area?"

"Oh sure, but mostly small ones, like diamond rings, bracelets, and lost money. I've dug up a few watches and hotel room keys. 'Course I always return 'em." The "pirate" puffed out his chest. "Me, I'm lookin' for big stuff. Well, I got to be movin' along. The name's White Beard." He put out his hand. "What's your handle?"

"Joe. Nice to meet you."

Joe watched as White Beard shuffled off, pushing his metal detector in front of him.

Just then he saw the two surfboards bouncing toward shore and waded in to retrieve them. He hurried to the hotel. Mr. Hardy and Mr. Drew were just arriving.

"Hi!" said Joe. "Anything new on the case?"

"No. I'm afraid not. How about you?" Mr. Drew replied.

"We may have a clue," Joe said, and told about Nancy's injury on the surfboard.

By this time, the group had reached Nancy's room. Hearing voices, they walked in. Nancy was propped up on the bed, with several pillows behind her. She had a stiff neck and a headache. Her injured forearm was resting on another pillow, and was wrapped in a towel with ice cubes enclosed.

"I'll be good as new tomorrow," Nancy reassured everyone.

She and Frank had been discussing the mean-looking young man whose surfboard had banged into hers. "I'm sure it wasn't an accident," Nancy said. "Do you think that the man is connected with the case and wanted to harm me so I couldn't hunt for the stolen treasure?"

"It sounds as if it's a good possibility," Mr. Hardy replied. "We know that the treasure is still on the island. No one has left without being searched. We think the thief simply reburied the treasure and is waiting until the heat is off before trying to leave the island."

Joe thought of White Beard and told the group his story. "Do you think there's any connection between him, the thief, and the treasure?"

"Could it be that Mr. Davison found White Beard's great-grandfather's treasure?" Frank asked.

"If so," Mr. Drew replied, "that old man is hunting in the wrong place. Mr. Davison found it a few miles inside the cove, not here on the beach."

"Unless," Mr. Hardy suggested, "White Beard knows the thief reburied it on our beach." He asked, "How about you young folks taking the metal detector we brought and using it out there tomorrow morning?"

"Good idea," Nancy responded. "But tell me exactly what we're looking for."

Her dad said, "A small metal chest filled with ancient Spanish gold coins and pieces of silver."

"Dad," Frank asked, "is there any identifying mark on the chest?"

"Yes," replied Mr. Hardy, "CAPTAIN HORATIO

RAMSEY, HAPPY SEA TRADER. Mr. Drew and I did some research and found that the ship, out of London, England, sank in a violent storm and all the men were lost. Later, it was rumored that three or four escaped in a small boat and got to this cove, then went inland and buried the treasure from the *Happy Sea Trader*."

Instantly, Joe wondered if Captain Ramsey could have been White Beard's great-grandfather. When he mentioned this, Nancy and Frank were eager to talk to him sometime soon. "We must try to find out where he lives," Nancy said. They decided to search him out the next day.

After breakfast, the three teenagers dressed in beach clothes and started out. Frank was carrying their new metal detector. Nancy gazed at it and asked, "How deep will it detect objects?"

"Two hundred feet, and it'll work under water as well as on land," Frank replied.

"Does the detector locate anything besides metal?" Nancy asked.

Joe grinned. "Fish, skeletons—you name it."

Frank added, "Maybe we'll find old Captain Ramsey's skeleton!"

"I'll stick to metal," Nancy declared. "Let's go!"

When the three detectives reached the

beach, Frank set down the detector and at once they could hear an insistent *beep, beep, beep.*

"Something's right under us! Nancy exclaimed, and immediately stuck her long-handled spade into the sand.

The boys began digging, too. Within a few minutes, they reached a depth of one foot. The detector was beeping wildly.

"A purse! A lady's evening bag!" Nancy announced, staring at the tarnished mesh bag with a chain handle.

The three young people had crouched down to study it when a flurry of sand behind them startled them. Joe looked up and was astounded to see a deeply tanned figure racing across the sand with the metal detector. In a flash, Joe was after him.

"Stop, you thief!" he cried out.

Frank and Nancy hurriedly filled in the hole they had just dug, so it was a moment before they could join in the chase. Then they raced off, with the lady's handbag swinging violently from side to side over Nancy's arm. She finally slipped it down inside her sweater blouse.

Meanwhile, Joe had run as fast as he could, but instead of the distance narrowing between himself and the detector thief, it was gradually widening. Suddenly, the fleet-footed stranger was stopped short by two men coming toward him. The thief dodged left and right, but the men grabbed him and held him tightly. One took away the metal detector.

Joe's heart sank. Were they, in turn, robbing the thief? Would the men perhaps jump into a car and zoom off? The detector might be gone forever! How would Nancy and the boys ever find the treasure?

Then Joe recognized the two men—they were his dad and Mr. Drew!

He reached them a minute later. "You caught the guy," he panted. "Who is he?"

Mr. Drew answered, "He won't say."

Joe looked hard at the black-haired, deeply suntanned thief. "He's the one who slammed into Nancy with his surfboard," he told the men.

"That's two counts against you," Mr. Hardy told the stranger. "What's your name?"

Silence.

"Okay," said Mr. Drew. "We'll introduce ourselves. This man is a famous detective—"

Hearing this, the black-haired man bolted, but Joe was after him in a flash and within seconds pinned him to the ground.

"Okay, I'm Juan Velasco. I ain't done nothin' wrong. That surfboard was an accident. I found the detector on the beach. How was I supposed to know it was yours?"

"That's enough," Mr. Drew told him. "Maybe the police chief will recognize you."

"Okay. I'll talk. Whadda you wanna know?"

Joe, less restrained than either his or Nancy's dad, blurted out, "I'll bet you're the guy who stole Mr. Davison's treasure!"

"That treasure didn't belong to him any more than it did to me."

Joe said, "I thought treasures were 'finder's keepers.'"

Mr. Drew remarked, "It belongs to the *first finder*, not to someone who steals it from him."

Juan looked confused, but said, "I ain't goin' to jail for takin' it, 'cause I ain't got it. I lost it!"

"How?" asked Joe. "Where?"

"Somewhere near shore. I was takin' it to the cave in the cove offshore about two miles. But the little chest was heavy. So was the shovel I had, and my surfboard, too. The boat capsized and the chest sank."

"Surely you hunted for it?" Mr. Drew asked.

"First thing next mornin', I was down here huntin'. Not a sign of my little chest," Juan replied. "That's why I go surfin' a lot, hopin' to see it gleamin' down there."

Joe spoke up. "And when you saw our strong

metal detector, you figured on using it to locate the treasure."

"Yeah. Hey, how about you guys lettin' me work with you?" He winked. "We could divide the profits."

Before Joe could reply, Mr. Drew said sternly, "You forget you're wanted as a thief. The treasure so far belongs to Mr. Davison."

"Yeah? Well, no two-bit detective can arrest me!" he said cockily.

Mr. Hardy remarked that there was a roadside phone not far away, and that he would go and check Juan's story with headquarters. He hurried off while the others waited. Mr. Drew asked Joe where Nancy and Frank were.

"I guess they're still on the beach. I was running so fast chasing this guy, I didn't wait for them."

As Frank sped with Nancy toward the road to follow Joe, she said, "Look who's coming!"

"White Beard!"

The old man, wearing his full pirate outfit, was pushing his small metal detector. Suddenly, he stopped, dropped to his knees, and began digging in the sand with his hands. He had noticed Nancy and Frank come up to him, but did not interrupt his work.

A minute later, he pulled out a silver dollar, stared at it, and chuckled. Aloud, he exclaimed, "White Beard, you can still do it!"

Nancy said, "Congratulations! That's great."

The old man looked up, startled, and quickly put the coin in his pocket. The two young people laughed, and Frank said, "We're friends of Joe's, the teenager you met on the beach last night. We'd like to talk to you. Would it be all right to visit you? It's about your great-grandfather's treasure."

"I live quite a piece from here at Clam Shell Point. But sure, come by anytime. And bring your friend Joe," White Beard said genially and then began hunting again.

Nancy and Frank hurried off. She asked, "Don't you hope it's his treasure?"

Frank nodded. "Kind of. I think he could use some money."

"I agree."

The two began to speculate on what had happened to Joe. By the time they reached the road, in the distance they could see him coming along with their dads, carrying the metal detector.

"Joe got it back!" Nancy exclaimed. "I wonder where the thief went?"

Her questions were answered in a few minutes, as they met the three who had caught the thief.

"The police came and picked him up," Joe explained. "His name is Juan Velasco. He confessed taking the old chest from Mr. Davison."

"Great!" said Frank. He looked at his dad and Mr. Drew. "Now all we have to do is find the treasure!"

Joe agreed. "Anybody know about the tides tomorrow? I want to get back to hunting."

Nancy pulled a tide table card from her sweater pocket. "Low tide tomorrow morning at eleven," she read.

"Let's start work at ten," Frank urged.

Nancy suddenly remembered that she had the gold evening bag under her sweater and pulled it out. "The boys and I dug this up," she explained to the men.

The gold had turned greenish from contact with the damp, salty sand.

"Can you open it?" Joe asked.

Nancy examined the bag. At first, she could not discover any way to unfasten it, but after letting her fingers move across the edges where a catch should be, she found a movable area. She pressed it hard and finally was able to pull the top of the bag apart.

Nancy fished in the bottom of the bag. The

leather lining had almost disintegrated but she felt a smaller, solid gold bag which opened with difficulty. The contents were dry. A white paper was wrapped around a large pearl. On the paper was written:

TO MY DARLING MARIA
FROM HORATIO R.

"Captain Horatio Ramsey!" Nancy exclaimed. "This must be from the treasure! I wonder who Maria was."

Mr. Drew looked at his daughter with a twinkle in his eyes. "How romantic! What will you do with it now?"

"I'm going to try finding a direct descendant of Maria."

"That's a bigger job than hunting for a needle in a haystack," Mr. Hardy commented. "But I wish you luck."

They all returned to the hotel and went to pick up their keys from the front desk. "Message for you, Miss Drew," the desk clerk said as he reached for her room key. He handed her a smudged envelope and said with a grin, "A pirate left this for you."

"Thank you," she said and quickly opened it.

Her companions watched her expression become excited.

To the obvious annoyance of the curious desk clerk, they walked out to a porch, which was deserted. Nancy showed them White Beard's note. It read:

DEAR MISS DREW:
I HAVE SOME INFO FOR YOU
ABOUT MY GREAT-GRANDPA.
YOU GOT TO COME OVER TO
MY SHACK. FOLLER THE
SOUTH BANK OF THE COVE
AND YOU WILL COME TO IT.
SEE MY FLAG.

"Sounds interesting," Mr. Hardy commented.

Nancy added, "Let's all go over there."

The metal detector was put away, and after freshening up, the group started out. Within ten minutes, the three teenagers were on their way to call on White Beard. They soon came in sight of the shack. It stood back from the water far enough to keep it from being washed away in a storm. A skull and crossbones pirate flag flew from a pole on the roof.

The visitors chuckled as they walked up to the door. White Beard was waiting and welcomed them with hearty handshakes. The walls of the one-room shack were covered completely with fishnets in which had been wedged photographs, shells, and skeletons or skulls of small sea creatures. On a crude wooden table in the center of the room lay several old-time albums and scrapbooks.

The elderly man was dressed in his pirate clothes but his feet were not bare. He now wore shiny, black leather boots.

"Ever eat shark meat?" he asked as they sat down, and produced a tin plate of black bread sandwiches.

He passed them around and though the visitors were wary of trying them, each one took a sandwich. When they did not bite into them, White Beard looked hurt. He took a big bite of his, and the others followed. To their amazement, they found the food delicious.

As they finished, Nancy said, "You mentioned a surprise for me."

"Oh, yes. I most forgot." White Beard opened one of the albums and pointed to the picture of a sea captain. Underneath was written HORATIO RAMSEY. "That was my great-grandpa on my mother's side," he announced proudly.

"That's terrific," Nancy said with a smile.

Frank asked, "Do you have a picture of your great-grandma?"

"Sure have," he replied, and turned several pages. "There she is. Pretty, ain't she? Came from Spain. Her name was Maria—Maria Ramsey."

The listeners gasped. What they had hoped might be true *was* true for certain! The treasure chest, if found, belonged to White Beard! Impulsively, Nancy opened the tote she carried and brought out the lady's gold bag, then turned to her friends with inquisitive eyes. They got the message and nodded slightly.

"White Beard," she said, handing the bag to him, "we think this belongs to you. I'll open the secret clasp. It's hard to work."

He looked at the group wonderingly and took out the smaller bag. When he saw the pearl and read the note, his eyes filled with tears. "My great-grandpa was goin' to give this to my great-grandma!" he said shakily. "You—you all found it buried?

"Yes," Nancy replied.

Joe added, "Thanks to our new super-duper detector. Now we hope to locate the rest of the treasure."

The visitors stood up to go. The old man was

too overcome to say anything but, "Thank you. Thank you kindly."

After the Drews and the Hardys were some distance from the shack, Mr. Drew said, "I think we should tell Mr. Davison at once of this new turn of events." Mr. Hardy agreed and the two men went off to talk to their client.

Nancy and the boys were up early the next morning to have breakfast several hours before their underwater search for the treasure chest. They carried both shallow and deep-sea diving equipment. When the three sleuths reached the beach, the only person on it was White Beard.

He grinned at them happily. "I just had to come out here and see how you make out. I'll be a-prayin' for you."

Frank asked him if he would guard the deep-sea paraphernalia. "'Deed I will," he replied.

After donning their face masks and flippers, the eager searchers hurried into the water, with Frank holding the detector. Instantly, the ocean seemed to be filled with sounds. The faint beeps from the metal detector were almost constant. Where should they start looking for the metal chest? The three swimmers surfaced and held a conference. They finally decided to change to the deep-sea gear and came ashore.

They told White Beard their plan.

"You be careful," he warned as they pulled on flippers and helmets and attached small oxygen tanks to their air hoses. To each of them, White Beard tied little sacks of shark-repellent powder. "You might need this," he said.

The young people had been told there was nothing which would repel a shark from attacking. "This here is a special concoction of mine," the elderly man urged.

Nancy, Frank, and Joe thanked him. Not wanting to hurt his feelings, they left the bags in place.

This time, the three sleuths swam out beyond the crashing waves and dived near the ocean floor. The detector was barely audible as they paralleled the shoreline for a while, then reversed their direction. Soon after crossing the spot in line with White Beard, they saw an object heading for them.

A shark!

The great, belligerent fish came with lightning speed. The swimmers were about to try dodging and doubling up their arms and legs to keep them from being bitten off when the shark suddenly swerved sideways and went off into deeper water. Apparently the repellent *had* worked!

At the same moment, the metal detector began beeping. As Nancy and Joe followed Frank, the sounds grew louder, then became almost deafening. Joe turned on the flashlight attached to his wrist. Directly beneath the swimmers lay a small, partially buried iron chest.

"The treasure!" Nancy exclaimed over the radio intercom.

She and the boys dug at it excitedly. The chest came loose. At this depth, it did not seem heavy, and Joe said he could carry it alone. But as the swimmers rose toward the surface, he said he needed help. Quickly, Nancy was at his side and together they brought the small chest to the beach. Frank came alongside carrying the detector.

Ready to greet them were White Beard, Mr. Drew, Mr. Hardy, and a stranger. The young people were helped out of their gear, then the man was introduced as Mr. Davison.

"Congratulations!" he said. "Yes, this is the chest I found, and now I understand it belongs to White Beard here."

The pirate was too overcome to speak. He just hugged the three young sleuths.

Joe said to them, "That shark repellent of yours saved our lives! We owe a lot to you."

Frank said, "Let's open the chest."

Mr. Davison, who had worked out the combination, had no trouble doing this. The chest was filled with valuable coins.

"It's a fortune!" White Beard exclaimed. "I don't need this. I'm a simple man."

He insisted that the lawyer and the detective be paid from the treasure. He would then give it to Mr. Davison for the museum.

Both Mr. Davison and White Beard requested that each of the three young detectives take five pieces as souvenirs of their gratitude to them.

As Frank chose his, he said, "This sure is my lucky day."

Joe grinned. "It's more fun than being eaten by a shark!"

Everyone looked at Nancy to hear what she would say. Her eyes twinkling, she made a deep curtsy to White Beard, and said, "This is my first gift from a pirate. I'll treasure it always. Thank you."

THE ARMORED LADY

The three young sleuths hurried through the airport corridor to the security checkpoint. Nancy Drew, in the lead, passed through the metal detector. Joe Hardy followed and they walked ahead quickly.

Frank Hardy had put down a small suitcase alongside his shoulder pack and gone to the end of the moving counter to collect them. The suitcase cleared but not the pack. A security guard stepped up to him.

"Follow me!" he ordered.

"Why, what's the matter?"

"The camera has detected a gun in your pack and I'll have to see some identification and a permit before you will be allowed to proceed."

"What! Well, I didn't put it there. I don't even own a gun!"

"You can explain to the police," the security guard said.

As other passengers stared, a second security officer appeared and took Frank to a small office. The unlocked pack was opened. Inside lay a cellophane bag containing a pistol. Frank stared in utter astonishment, as the officer said, "You're under arrest!"

Meanwhile, Nancy and Joe, waiting in the boarding lounge, wondered what had delayed Frank. "We'll miss our plane," Nancy said, glancing at her wristwatch.

Joe walked over to the desk where seat passes for the flight were given out. He asked the attendant to phone the security checkpoint and find out what had happened to his brother. He was amazed at the terse report he received.

"Let me speak to my brother, please," he requested, and was transferred to the office where Frank was being held. "Frank! What happened?"

"Listen, Joe. You and Nancy go on to Newkirk. I'll meet you there. The police here are getting in touch with Dad and Chief Collig." In the background, Frank could hear an announcement: "Final boarding, Flight 206."

"Hurry, Joe! I'll be okay."

His brother did not argue, but hung up the phone, rushed up to Nancy, and said, "Let's go! Tell you everything later." The two raced along the ramp to the plane.

"The third one in our group isn't coming," Nancy explained to the hostess.

During the flight, she and Joe talked worriedly about their dilemma. How had the gun gotten into Frank's bag?

"And why?" Nancy asked. "Joe, do you think it could have anything to do with the mystery we've been asked to work on?"

"You mean to delay our going there?"

"Yes. Even to keep us from going," Nancy replied. "And Cousin Nell really needs us."

The couple continued their discussion about the Newkirk mystery. It concerned an old, spooky opera house which was still being used. Recently, strange and dangerous things had been happening during performances, and attendance had fallen off. So far, the police had been unsuccessful in their investigation, so a committee of the subscribers had been formed to help find a new way to solve the mystery.

Nancy's dad's cousin, Mrs. Nell Bancroft, was the chairperson and had asked Nancy, Frank, and Joe to come stay with her and, she hoped, crack the case.

As soon as the plane reached Newkirk, Joe rushed to a phone and called the security office where his brother had been detained. A few minutes later, he rejoined Nancy, a broad grin on his face.

"Frank's okay!" he exclaimed. "Not pounding on cell bars! He'll be here in an hour."

Nancy smiled. "Great! What about the gun?"

"It was confiscated. The strange thing about it is that it's a stage gun!"

"A stage gun!" Nancy exclaimed. "You mean it only can fire blanks?"

"That's what the police told Frank. Since the gun is harmless, they decided to release him. There was just time for him to catch the next plane, so he didn't wait to learn anything more."

"Well, while we're waiting why don't we go get our luggage?" Nancy suggested.

The two sleuths went to the baggage-claim section. Luggage from their plane was just coming onto the rotary receiving platform.

They watched carefully for their bags. When they came out on the conveyor belt, Joe rushed to pick them up. Then suddenly, one man grabbed a large suitcase. As he turned to leave, the stranger turned quickly and bumped into Nancy. For a couple of seconds, he stared at her, a startled expression on his face. Then he muttered, "Sorry," and hurried off.

Nancy wondered if the encounter meant anything. The stranger seemed to recognize her. In her mind, she repeated a description of the man—medium height, auburn hair, brown, beady eyes, soft voice. Wore a dark suit, shirt, and tie. Carried a black bag as well as the large suitcase.

The other baggage claimants dispersed. Joe and Nancy decided to have a snack in one of the airport's coffee shops while waiting for Frank. After they had ordered their ice-cream sundaes, Nancy told Joe about the incident with the stranger.

"That does sound suspicious, but it could be nothing," Joe said. Nancy agreed but said she would keep the description of the man in mind.

The hour seemed to pass quickly as they continued to discuss the day's events. Frank's plane was on time and he quickly emerged from it, so the three sleuths were soon together in a taxi headed for Mrs. Nell Bancroft's home.

"I'm so glad you're going to stay with me," the pleasant, gray-haired woman said when they arrived. "My husband is away on business, and I'll feel safer with three detectives in the house." She chuckled.

"And in the opera house also?" Nancy asked.

"Yes, there too. I'm confident you'll solve the mystery. It's really been a nightmare for us, and especially for Mr. Endicott."

"Who's Mr. Endicott?" asked Nancy.

"Mr. Avery Endicott is our largest stockholder. And has been ever since he was an actor here himself years ago. Mr. Endicott telephoned last week to say that if the theater continues to lose business, he thinks we should seriously consider closing down."

"Is there anything more you can tell us about it?" asked Frank, as the group sat down in her attractive, antique-furnished living room.

"There's really nothing more to tell. Perhaps you should attend the performance tonight. Of course, I hope nothing happens, but if it does, it'll be good that you're there."

When Nancy mentioned making a reservation, Mrs. Bancroft smiled. "That won't be necessary. These days the old opera house is never filled. I'm afraid if the spook isn't caught soon, the old Newkirk landmark will have to close," her cousin said sadly.

"And a lot of singers will be out of work," Nancy commented.

"I'm afraid so."

Frank spoke up, "Mrs. Bancroft, you mentioned a spook. Do you think someone is playing spook?"

Her reply was, "I'm not superstitious and I'm sure the opera house isn't haunted. Therefore a person, or persons, are responsible for causing the trouble."

"But why?" Joe asked.

The woman shrugged helplessly. "I can't imagine why anyone would do such a thing."

That evening, Nancy, Frank, and Joe arrived at the huge opera house early. It was a cool evening and the vast, dimly lighted structure was not heated.

"The temperature in here is just right for a chiller thriller," Joe remarked.

"Spine-chilling," Frank agreed, and playfully turned up his jacket collar and thrust both hands in his pockets.

Frank bought tickets for seats in the third row. As the three sleuths walked down the long aisle, they observed the two tiers of empty boxes with velvet curtains at the rear. Great hiding places, Nancy thought. Anybody could enter one of the boxes and throw an object onto the stage or into the orchestra pit.

Frank turned and observed the empty balcony and the gallery above it. What perfect places for a person with a warped mind to slump in a seat and plan some evil deed!

Joe's eyes were focused on the images in the fresco bordering the stage just above the mammoth velvet curtain. There were white plaster figures of sad clowns, obese men with silly grins, a ghostly woman, and a devil wearing a half-mask and a cloak thrown back from the shoulders.

As Nancy sat down between the boys, she whispered, "I'd love to see what's under the stage—the dressing rooms, the costumes. Maybe my cousin could arrange a tour for us."

"Great idea," said Frank. "We might find some clues to the mystery down there."

Slowly, men and women trickled into the opera house. Members of the orchestra took their places in the pit and began the overture to *Carmen.* Suddenly, there was a scream backstage.

The scream made the audience nervous. Several people left their seats, but in the lobby were urged by ushers to return. When the overture ended, the manager came out in front of the curtain to speak. "I regret to announce that Señorita Torres has been taken ill suddenly. Tonight her part will be sung by Miss Elizabeth Miller." At once, there was an undercurrent of disappointment. Señorita Torres was a great favorite with the crowd.

The man walked off, and almost immediately the orchestra started to play, the curtain went up, and the chorus burst into song. Nancy was intrigued not only by the stirring music, but by the colorful costumes of the crowd and the set depicting a square in Seville, Spain.

Nevertheless, her mind kept reverting to the scream. Was there any connection between it and the star's illness? Had *she* screamed? Or someone else? I must find out, the girl detective determined.

During intermission, the three sleuths asked the ushers and at the box office for an explanation, but none of them offered one.

"If they know," Joe said, "they're not telling!"

After the performance was over, the trio tried to go backstage but were not permitted to do so. Security had been tightened since the strange occurrences had plagued the opera house.

"I'll ask my cousin if she can get permission for us to go backstage tomorrow," Nancy volunteered.

A tour was indeed arranged for the following afternoon, as no performance was scheduled for that evening.

The eager detectives were prompt. A guard admitted them. "Look around as long as you like." He winked. "And find the ghost!" He showed them the enormous panel which held the switches for the hundreds of lights. Each was marked.

Joe asked, "Does the ghost work at other times than during performances?"

"I guess so. We've found pieces of scenery that have been ruined by fresh paint from our storeroom. That could not have happened when a lot of people were here."

Frank asked, "Who screamed just before last night's performance?"

"That was Señorita Torres, right before she fainted and couldn't go on."

Nancy spoke up. "Did she say anything?"

"Yes. She said, 'There it is! The ghost!' We didn't see anyone, but she'd been looking up at the cage where a stagehand sometimes sits."

Nancy inquired about the singer's health, and was relieved to learn the actress was recovering from her temporary shock. "But nobody can see the señorita or interview her," the guard replied.

The young people wandered around, but presently the guard said the place was closing. "Come back any other time," he invited.

The visitors left but said they would return the next day. When Mrs. Bancroft heard the story of the latest incident and her guests' request to investigate the opera house further, she was glad to comply. Directly after breakfast the following morning, the necessary arrangements were made.

"You can investigate the place any time after ten o'clock. Usually there are no tours until afternoon. Go to the stage door and ring the bell three times."

They did as she instructed and were admitted by the guard who had spoken to them the day before. He told them his name was Wilbur. Nancy inquired about Señorita Torres and learned she was still in a highly nervous state.

Frank asked, "Any news about the ghost?"

"None," Wilbur replied. "If anybody was up near that cage, he'd have to have wings to get there. The cable that operated it has been broken for two years. We keep a sturdy chest under it, so if the cage should drop, it won't hurt anyone."

The group had just turned their backs on the area when they heard a snap, followed by a crash. The cage had dropped, smashing the chest!

"Oh!" the startled group exclaimed, looking upward to see if anybody was visible among the rafters. No one was in sight.

Wilbur looked relieved. "I'm glad this didn't

happen during a performance. The singers are edgy enough as it is. If you don't mind, I'd appreciate it if you don't breathe a word about what happened." The visitors promised.

The noise of the crash had brought several employees of the opera house to the scene. They too were pledged to secrecy and helped remove the cage to an inconspicuous spot in the wings.

Among the group was a dark-skinned, middle-aged woman who introduced herself as Aunt Martha Santos, the wardrobe mistress. "Would you like to come to the basement and see the costumes?"

"Yes, indeed," the visitors chorused.

Wilbur called over, "Watch your step, Martha. These young folks are detectives, come to solve our mystery."

Aunt Martha chuckled. "Follow me."

She took them down a creaky stairway to a vast, partially lighted area filled with rows and rows of cases containing hundreds of men's and women's suits, dresses, and accessories.

Joe pointed to one and took out a cane. "Anybody need a cane? How much am I bid for this English walking stick?" he joked.

On dozens of shelves were hats of all varieties—top hats, bowlers, and fedoras with long, colored feathers. Aunt Martha put one on

Frank's head. He immediately made a sweeping bow, swinging the fedora in a great half-circle.

The wardrobe mistress picked up an ornate, three-tiered, Asiatic hat and set it on Nancy's head. It was so heavy the slender girl's knees buckled, and laughing, she said, "No thanks. I don't want to play the part of an ancient queen!"

Frank had noticed a wired enclosure with a door and asked what was inside.

"That's our armor room," Aunt Martha replied, clicking a switch to turn on the inside lights. "There are suits of armor from various periods of history and many countries of Europe, Asia, and the Orient. I'll show them to you." She unlocked the door with a key from her pocket.

The three sleuths were astounded by the collection. Each armored figure stood on a low platform. The room gleamed with the shiny metal. Aunt Martha explained in which operas certain suits were used.

"They must weigh a ton," Joe commented.

"Most of them do," she agreed, then asked, "Did you ever hear of the Armored Lady?"

"No," the visitors answered, and Nancy asked, "Is her suit here?"

"Yes, it is. I'll show you. The suit of armor is

smaller than any of the others, although you will notice that most of the figures are short. In many countries, men of olden times were much smaller than the average man is today."

The three visitors followed her to a corner where the Armored Lady stood. Nancy said, "Wasn't it unusual for women to wear armor? They never went to war or fought in jousts."

"That's true," Aunt Martha replied, "but here's the story of the Armored Lady. In medieval times, a couple were madly in love. When the man was to be sent to war, the woman couldn't bear the thought of being away from him. She declared she was going with him, then secretly had a suit of armor made and went along. He was killed and she was caught by the enemy. They took her suit and said it would be given to a man. She was so angry and unhappy that she put a curse on the suit!"

"What was it?" Joe asked.

"That if any man ever wore it, something awful would happen to him."

"And did it?" Frank queried.

"Yes. There are many stories of men who met strange deaths in that suit. Finally, it was put in a museum. Last year, at an auction of Old World objects, the Newkirk Opera House bought it, and I think that's when our bad luck began."

Nancy asked, "Has any singer here ever worn the Armored Lady's suit?"

"Funny you should ask that," said Aunt Martha. "Tomorrow one of our basses plans to wear this suit. He's not a bit superstitious and is small enough to fit into the armor. You ought to come and hear him. He has a gorgeous voice." She chuckled. "He's so little I don't know where it comes from!"

"We'll be here," Frank told the wardrobe mistress, and the others nodded.

As they were leaving the room, Nancy spotted a key lying on the floor by the door. To her surprise, the name on the tag attached to it was Avery Endicott's!

"How could this have gotten here?" Joe asked. "I heard that Mr. Endicott hasn't been here in ages!"

"But he was an actor here once." Frank said thoughtfully. "Perhaps whoever took his pass-key also 'borrowed' a prop as well—the gun that was found in my bag!"

The three detectives discussed the new development on the way to Nell Bancroft's. They decided not to mention the clue to anyone until they had pieced it together with the information they already had.

When they arrived at Mrs. Bancroft's, she had

some news for Nancy, Frank, and Joe.

"Mr. Endicott just telephoned. He said he'd like me to set up a meeting to discuss the closing of the theater with the other stockholders and board members," Mrs. Bancroft said sadly. "I was so hoping it wouldn't come to this!"

"Well, we still have some time. Maybe there's a chance to save the theater," Frank said, and proceeded to tell Mrs. Bancroft the story of the Armored Lady. "Tomorrow evening we're going to a performance to keep an eye on the bass singer who will wear the suit," Frank explained. "None of us believes the story about the curse put on the suit, but if something goes wrong, we'll be here to watch for clues.

"Good thinking," Mrs. Bancroft praised the three young people. "Well, I hope you catch the ghost."

The following evening, the three sleuths purchased seats in the front row in order to watch every movement in the orchestra pit and on the stage. Partway through the first act of Verdi's *Macbeth,* a column of soldiers in armor marched in, singing a stirring melody. They were led by a short man playing the part of Banquo, who soon broke into a bass solo.

"That must be the Armored Lady's suit," Nancy whispered.

"That's some voice," Frank commented.

Suddenly, in the middle of a phrase, the bass grasped his throat and stopped singing. The next moment he ran into the wings. The young people could see him tear off his helmet and breastplate. Then he disappeared. The curtain was rung down, leaving the audience stunned.

"What happened?" "Is he ill?" "I told you this place has an evil ghost in it," were some of the remarks that could be heard.

Joe leaned over to his companions. "It looks as if the curse is working."

Presently, the manager stepped out in front of the curtain. "Ladies and gentlemen, we regret the interruption and ask your patience during a brief intermission. We will resume the performance shortly."

There was a buzz of conversation throughout the audience as everyone speculated on what had caused the man to stop singing and dash off.

Frank said, "Nancy, you keep watch here. Joe, follow me."

He quickly stepped across the barrier in front of him into the orchestra pit. Joe followed. The musicians had already gone through the opening into the basement. Frank led the way directly to the armor room. The bass, minus his costume, was gargling as the wardrobe mistress and the manager looked on.

"Is your voice coming back?" Aunt Martha asked the young man, as he rested a moment.

"Y-yes," he said, and a few minutes later tried some scales. A look of relief came over everyone's face.

Frank asked, "May I examine the Armored Lady's suit?"

Aunt Martha answered the boy. "Do you think it was responsible for the soloist's losing his voice?"

"Possibly."

"Then go ahead."

Frank and Joe looked thoroughly through the helmet, which had a visor that could be raised and lowered. They found no foreign objects, but Joe insisted the helmet had a peculiar odor.

"I suspect someone put a spray in there recently," he declared, and walked over to the singer to ask him.

"Yes, I did notice a faint odor, then suddenly my throat became absolutely dry and I could not sing." He insisted he was all right to go on stage, but he would wear a different suit of armor.

Finally, the curtain went up and the opera continued. There were many curtain calls at the end, especially for the singer who had been stricken.

Nancy was intrigued by the story of the Armored Lady's suit.

"So the curse worked again," she said as the three sleuths rode home. "I'm sure the opera house ghost is responsible. I'd like to come here tomorrow when there will be no rehearsals or a performance, and hide in the armor room—even wear the Armored Lady's suit, and watch."

Frank and Joe looked concerned. "That could be very dangerous, Nancy. Are you sure you want to do it?"

"I think it's the only chance we have of solving this mystery," she said seriously.

"But what makes you think the ghost will be coming to the armor room?" Joe asked.

Nancy replied, "We know he works on the stage and under it, and the only way to get backstage is through the armor room. He's bound to show up. We'll have to take the wardrobe mistress into our confidence and get her to help us."

"How about the guard?" Frank asked. "Let's ask him who besides himself and Aunt Martha has a key to the building."

The eager sleuths started early for the mysterious building. The guard admitted them. In answer to Frank's question, he said only three others had a key to the main door: the chairman of the board of governors, Aunt Martha, and the night guard, who was a very trustworthy man. Wilbur further explained that only he and the night guard had a key to the stage door.

Frank asked him if it would be possible for a stranger to slip in with the actors.

"Oh, no. Of course I don't always recognize all of them, but each singer and stagehand has a pass which must be shown."

The three detectives went directly to Aunt Martha's little workroom. She was busy mending a dancer's costume which had been ripped.

"Good morning," she said. "You're early. You look excited. Some new plan to catch the ghost?"

"Yes," Nancy whispered in case any eavesdroppers were listening, or the place had been bugged. She confided the whole story and the wardrobe mistress agreed to cooperate. "I know plenty of places to hide."

Joe grinned and added in a barely audible voice, "When Frank sings, you give the alarm for the police." She nodded.

Aunt Martha unlocked the door to the armor room.

Nancy requested a cloth and pail of water to cleanse the helmet, in case Joe's suspicion of a chemical spray's having caused the soloist to lose his voice was correct.

"I have already done that," the wardrobe mistress told her. "Directly after use, each garment is cleaned."

She unlocked the door and the detectives went to work inspecting the inside of every suit. They found nothing unusual about them and practiced getting into the suits. Each sleuth wondered how long it would be before the "ghost" would appear. Suddenly, something heavy crashed on the stage overhead.

The waiting sleuths did not move. They figured that perhaps the ghost had caused the noise to attract attention to the stage while he went below into the gloomy wardrobe area. Presently, they heard soft footfalls and a flashlight was beamed toward the armor room.

In a few moments, a man came to the door, unlocked it, and tiptoed inside. Immediately, he took several small white envelopes from a pocket and deftly began to hide them under pieces of the segmented armor, attaching them with tape.

After the man had planted nearly fifty of them, he accidentally turned the flashlight so it shone directly on his face. Nancy stifled a gasp. He was the man who had bumped into her at the airport!

It was time to act, she decided. The Armored Lady stepped down from the platform and walked toward him. At the same moment, Joe in his armored suit dashed for the doorway to prevent the stranger's escape. From another metal warrior came an operatic, rousing "O Sole Mio." The wardrobe mistress heard it and ran from her hiding place. She quickly phoned the police.

The crook tried hard to get away, but was no match for three young people in suits of armor with metal gauntlets. When he was subdued, they took off the warriors' gear.

"Who are you?" Frank asked their prisoner.

"None of your business."

"Pretty soon it will be police business," said Joe. The man winced but said nothing.

Nancy decided to make a wild guess. "You're working for Avery Endicott. You're part of a smuggling ring."

The man made a dash for the door, but Frank and Joe were there to stop him.

"You three are too good for me. I thought our plan was perfect!" the criminal admitted dejectedly. "Avery and I used to work together in the theater, but when we couldn't get work, we got in on this smuggling scheme. Avery thought this place was great for storing the stuff, but knew he'd be recognized if he showed up here. He gave me a blueprint and now I know every inch of this old opera house. So does Avery. We planned to make the place so spooky no one would attend performances and we'd have the place to ourselves."

"But meanwhile," Frank said, "you were going to use the armor and sell the stuff as you got orders. How did you know about us?"

"Nell Bancroft told Avery the committee's plan to use you. We decided to follow you and Avery sent me to watch you boys. I followed you to the airport and sat next to you. I slipped the stage gun that Avery had from the old days into your bag while you were busy talking, so you'd be delayed, maybe arrested. I didn't want you in the way."

Just then, they heard voices and footsteps coming down the hall. Four policemen arrived with Aunt Martha. After learning the story, they praised the three sleuths, then left with their prisoner, saying they would have Avery Endicott apprehended at once.

As Aunt Martha helped set the armor in place, she said, "The board of governors ought to give you folks a big banquet and a great big reward for solving the mystery of our old opera house."

"No, thanks," the three sleuths chorused, and decided to leave Newkirk that evening.

When Mrs. Bancroft drove them to the airport, Nancy did several stretching exercises. "I certainly felt cramped in that metal suit," she said. "The real Armored Lady must have been a toy soldier!"

THE INTERLOCKING MAZE

The audience in the theater of the River Heights Amusement Park held its breath as the team of young gymnasts climbed higher and higher, forming a pyramid. Frank Hardy was one of the anchormen, while his brother Joe was alone at the top of the five-tiered formation.

"Suppose one of them should fall!" said a nervous woman onlooker. "The whole pyramid might collapse!" She closed her eyes to shut out the sight.

"Oh my goodness, look what they're doing now!" exclaimed Mrs. Hannah Gruen, the Drews' housekeeper, who was seated with Nancy and her father.

Each pyramider locked one arm and one leg with the boy on his left or right. The final result looked like a huge, interlocking fence.

"Magnificent!" Mr. Drew said, applauding loudly.

As Nancy clapped, she remarked, "I had no idea the Bayport High gym team was so good."

When the Drews heard that the group had been engaged for a week of performances in River Heights, they had invited Frank and Joe to stay with them.

Hannah Gruen was still applauding. She said, "I don't see how those boys are ever going to get their arms and legs untangled!"

The gymnasts unwound, then Joe made his way down two tiers and jumped the rest of the way. In seconds, all the performers were standing on the stage, taking bows. Since it was the final act for the night, the boys changed clothes, then followed the Drews home in their own car.

When they arrived, Nancy congratulated them. Then she asked, her eyes twinkling, "What kind of pyramid are you—Egyptian or South American? And were you once made out of stone?"

"Oh, sure!" Joe replied, "and we came to life after a thousand years just to see how your sleuthing is going."

Over cups of hot chocolate, sandwiches, and cake at the dining room table, Mr. Drew said,

"You boys arrived just in time to help Nancy solve a mystery."

"What kind of mystery?" Frank asked, intrigued at once.

"It concerns a girl, Marilyn Everett, whose father struck it rich in the oil fields but sold out. He died soon afterward and left all his money to Marilyn. Immediately, her father's half brother showed up. He claims Marilyn's father borrowed a lot of money from him and is demanding that Marilyn pay it back. This man, Roscoe Everett, was a wild teenager, and was always embarrassing the family. Marilyn is sure he never lent any money to her father."

"Where do Marilyn and her uncle live?" Joe asked.

"Marilyn," Nancy replied, "lives just outside of town. I'm not sure where her uncle is staying at the moment. He's generally been a drifter, and has threatened her many times. She's afraid to stay alone, so I've invited her to come here tomorrow and remain until the case is settled."

At that moment, the telephone rang. Nancy wondered who would be calling at such a late hour. She hurried to answer. A frightened voice said, "Nancy, someone's here from Uncle Roscoe. Says if I don't sign—"

Next came a scream. The caller's phone was

restored to its cradle. Instantly, Nancy dialed Marilyn's number. There was no answer.

Nancy rushed back to the dining room and said, "Marilyn's in trouble. We'd better get right out to her house."

"Shall I call the police?" Hannah Gruen asked.

Mr. Drew said, "Yes, but we'll leave right away. We can get there faster. I know a short-cut."

The lawyer and the three young sleuths whizzed away in his car. Arriving at the Everett home, they found it in darkness.

"Do you think Marilyn was forced to go with the intruder?" Frank suggested. "And how are we going to get in?"

"She gave me a key," Mr. Drew replied.

The group hurried inside the house, turned on lights, and began a hunt for Marilyn. They divided forces and looked everywhere—in closets, under beds, in the basement, in the attic. Marilyn was not in the house.

"She must have been kidnapped!" Joe declared. "Where do we go from here?"

No one answered him. They stood in silence for several seconds, each one trying to figure out the best way to proceed. Suddenly, the telephone rang. Nancy, nearest it, picked up the receiver.

"Yes?"

"Nancy, this is Hannah. Come home. Marilyn is here!"

"Really?" Nancy exclaimed. "How'd she get there?"

"Drove herself. She's pretty upset. I must get back to her. Good-bye."

To the astonishment of the others, Nancy explained what had happened. They all left immediately for the Drew home.

When they reached the house, the attractive, twenty-one-year-old girl was introduced, then she told them the full story. Her uncle had sent a messenger with a paper for her to sign. When she delayed doing so, he threatened to harm her.

"I said I'd have to get a pen. Instead I called you, Nancy, but he followed me and grabbed the phone. I ran out the back door, got in my car, and drove off. I was afraid he might guess I was coming here, so I drove around town to lose him. I was a wreck when I arrived. Mrs. Gruen, bless her heart, helped me calm down and gave me some hot tea. I feel better now."

"But what a scare!" Hannah commented. "I

think we should all try to get some sleep."

There was no disturbance during the night and by morning Marilyn felt much more relaxed. She insisted upon going home to get her clothes.

"Frank, Joe, and I will go with you," Nancy said. Out of earshot of Marilyn, she whispered to the boys, "I think we should see if that man came back last night to take anything, especially papers of Mr. Everett's for Uncle Roscoe to use in his claims."

When the four young people reached Marilyn's home, she looked around, then declared that nothing had been stolen.

"May we see your father's desk?" Nancy asked. "My dad has some of Mr. Everett's papers. He collected them when we decided to take the case. We'd like to take a look at what's left."

Marilyn led the way to her father's den on the first floor, and opened drawer after drawer of the big mahogany flattop desk. Nancy and the boys riffled through papers and receipts of bills, but found no personal letters.

"Marilyn," said Frank, "did your father keep any letters and personal stationery somewhere else?"

"Yes, over in this little cabinet." She walked

to a wooden, ornate piece, opened the top drawer, and gasped.

"All the stationery is gone!"

"I was afraid of that!" Frank told her. "He can use that stationery to forge letters from your father. We must tell Mr. Drew at once. But first let's see if the letters are missing."

Marilyn opened the two other drawers. "Everything has been taken!" she cried out.

"What did the messenger look like?" Joe asked her.

"He was a huge man and ugly—reminded me of a gorilla."

Nancy phoned her father to report the latest findings, then the group left. Frank and Joe had to report early at the amusement park for their daily show, but said they had time to show the girls around, and perhaps take one of the rides.

"Would you rather not, Marilyn?" Nancy asked.

"I'll come, but I'm afraid I'm not in a very happy mood," the girl replied.

The park was nearly deserted, as it was still early in the day. Frank bought tickets to the giant roller coaster. It had been in operation for many years and still used the cog cable to pull up the cars, which then whizzed down the track at breakneck speed.

The four young people were the only ones boarding the ride. A car with two double seats came along and stopped. Marilyn climbed into the back, with Frank following.

"You're going to miss half the thrill," said Joe as he and Nancy sat down in the front seat. They strapped themselves in and the car started with a jerk. Up the incline it went. As the car reached the top, Marilyn looked down and gasped.

"You'll be perfectly safe," Frank assured her.

"It's not that," she said. "I saw my awful uncle down there! What's he doing here?"

Before she could point him out to the others, the car started downward, gathering tremendous speed as it advanced. Marilyn clung to Frank. Joe put an arm around Nancy. The rush of wind blew their hair straight backward and tingled their faces.

The car zoomed nearly to the top of another rise, then almost seemed to stop. A look of alarm came over the riders' faces. Would their roller coaster roll backward down the slope and maybe crash into an oncoming car?

Fortunately, the cable was there as a safety precaution, and the car's "feet" reached down to grab the cogs. The two-seater did not move.

Nancy looked at the track. "The cable isn't running!" she whispered to Joe.

They waited for it to renew operation, but nothing happened. Five minutes went by, then ten. Finally, over the loudspeaker came an announcement: "There will be a one-hour delay. The management is sorry."

Frank and Joe looked at each other and Joe exclaimed, "That'll make us too late for our special performance! The governor is coming to see our pyramid formation!"

Nancy smiled. "How about your climbing down the framework of this roller coaster? That should be easy for two pyramiders."

"And leave you girls alone?" Frank objected.

Marilyn said, "We'll be all right. Go ahead."

The Hardys argued for a few minutes, then climbed out of the car. They started their descent from one crosspiece of each metal bar to another. At a certain point, it was necessary for them to drop from one handhold to another.

"Oh!" Marilyn exclaimed, fearful they would lose their grip and crash down. Finally, they made it safely, waved up at the girls, then hurried away.

Nancy and Marilyn settled back to wait, but within ten minutes the girl detective became restless. "Marilyn," she said, "would you dare try going down the way the boys did?"

Her companion paled. "Oh, I don't know. I never climbed anything but a tree or a ladder."

She surveyed the intricate framework, and finally said, "I can do it hand over hand. If we take it slowly and don't try dropping from one bar to another, I'm willing to try. But suppose my uncle is down there, or that awful man who works with him, and he harms us?"

"We'll have to take that chance, unless you'd rather sit up here for an hour or more."

"Let's go."

Nancy started off first, grabbing a nearby slanting steel beam. Since there was no underpinning, she went along hand over hand, clutching tightly until she came to the next upright. There Nancy waited for Marilyn. The two went on down until they came to the spot where Frank and Joe had dropped to the bar below.

"I can't do it," Marilyn declared.

The young sleuth pondered the situation. Even if she took the chance, she knew Marilyn would not. And I couldn't leave the poor girl stranded up here, she told herself.

Just then, Nancy saw a workman not far away. "Help!" she cried out. "Help!"

He gazed upward and a look of disbelief came over his face.

"How'd you get there?" he shouted.

"Our car is stuck up top," Nancy replied. "Please get us a long ladder. Quickly!"

The man turned and ran off. In a few minutes, he was back with another worker and an extension ladder. The girls were out of their predicament in seconds.

"You must be crazy to pull a stunt like that," growled the assistant. "Who are you, anyway?"

Nancy gave her name, then said, "This is Marilyn Everett."

"Everett, eh?" the first man said. "Any relation to Roscoe Everett?"

Marilyn, startled, replied, "He's my uncle. You know him?"

"Just from being around here. He owns part of this amusement park."

"What!" Marilyn exclaimed. "I—I thought he was poor!" she blurted. "He claims—"

Nancy grabbed the girl's arm to warn her not to say any more.

"Yes?" the workman prodded. "He claims what?"

Nancy smiled at the man. "Oh, it's just a family matter. You wouldn't be interested. Come on, Marilyn, let's go. And many thanks to you for rescuing us."

The girls hurried off. Instead of heading for her car, Nancy led the way to the theater. The boys had just finished their pyramid act and were being congratulated by the governor.

As they said good-bye, Frank and Joe spotted

the two girls and hurried to meet them. "The roller coaster must have been fixed in a hurry," Frank said.

Nancy shook her head and her eyes twinkled. "You're not the only ones who can climb down framework."

"You didn't!" Joe gasped.

"If we hadn't," Nancy went on, "we wouldn't have picked up a valuable clue."

"Tell us," Frank urged.

Nancy related the story, and Marilyn asked, "If Uncle Roscoe has money, why does he have to pretend my father owed him some?"

Frank suggested that Uncle Roscoe might be in some kind of trouble unrelated to the amusement park and in need of money. What easier way to get it than from his brother's estate?

"Let's find out why the roller coaster stopped running," Joe suggested. "Maybe he did it on purpose to keep us from doing any sleuthing."

At the starting gate, the group learned that someone—a big, burly man—had damaged the electrical system with a huge hammer, and run off before he could be caught. Electricians were working to restore power. The sleuths wondered if he could have been the intruder at Marilyn's house the night before!

As the young people turned away, Marilyn said, "I believe Uncle Roscoe is behind this. He wants to harm me, or at least intimidate me." The others agreed.

Nancy asked one of the workmen where Mr. Everett's office was. "I think at the Crystal Maze," he replied.

Frank checked the time. "Let's have an early lunch, then go to the Crystal Maze before Joe and I have to report at the theater. We have to rehearse a new routine for tonight's performance."

Everyone was in favor of the plan, and went to the refreshment stand. The three sleuths ate heartily, but Marilyn hardly touched her food. Nancy took the girl's hand and squeezed it. "Marilyn, try to cheer up. I'm sure we'll solve your mystery."

"Oh, you have to. I'm so frightened."

Joe, who could not stand to see anyone in such distress, doubled up his fists and said dramatically, "Just let me get hold of that man!"

Marilyn smiled. "I'm so lucky to have you helping me," she said.

The four hurried off to the Crystal Maze. Nancy asked the girl at the ticket window where she could find Mr. Roscoe Everett.

"I dunno. Want tickets?"

"That all depends," Nancy replied. "When will Mr. Everett be here?"

"I dunno. You want tickets or don't you?"

Nancy ignored the question. "Where is Mr. Everett's office?"

"Say, who are you? I'm here to sell tickets, not to answer a lotta questions."

Nancy knew there was no use arguing with such an uncooperative girl. She would have to find out for herself. She nodded to her companions, so Frank bought tickets. The four went inside the maze.

The narrow corridor was lined on both sides with full-length mirrors, and even the ceiling was made of glass. There were many twists and turns.

"Wow, this sure is a maze!" Joe exclaimed, as he bumped into his own image in an offset of the corridor. When he backed out, Frank was approaching and thought his brother was going forward. They crashed and both of them went down.

"This isn't exactly brotherly love," Joe quipped as he stood up.

"If this keeps up," Frank remarked, "you and I won't be much good to the pyramiders!"

Meanwhile, Nancy and Marilyn had gone ahead, intent upon finding a door to Roscoe

Everett's office. They saw none and emerged from the maze.

"Perhaps we were given the wrong information about where my uncle stays," Marilyn suggested.

In a few minutes, the Hardys joined them, confirming that there was no visible door to any room which opened off the glass corridor. Adding that they must hurry to join the other pyramiders, the Hardys trotted off.

Nancy said to Marilyn, "Before we go, let's look on the rear wall of the building. There may be a door." Again, however, the girls were disappointed. Nancy saw a small opening and thought it might be a keyhole, but discovered that it was too small. After searching for a few more minutes, they left for home.

At dinner that evening, Mr. Drew made a surprise announcement. "I had a phone call from Roscoe Everett. He said he'll soon have the necessary papers to prove his claim."

"Oh!" Marilyn exclaimed. "Suppose—"

Nancy asked, "Dad, do you think Marilyn's uncle found something in that cabinet which he'll use to prove his contention?"

"That's possible, but I thought I had removed everything pertaining to the case."

"Uncle Roscoe will probably use some of the

stationery missing from the cabinet to show you his 'proof,'" Nancy said.

Her father nodded, then asked Marilyn if she had a sample of her uncle's handwriting.

"No. He always phoned."

Frank and Joe said they had to leave for the theater for that evening's performance. They had just left when the Drew telephone rang. Nancy answered and was surprised to find that the call was for Marilyn from Uncle Roscoe! As Marilyn was about to pick up the receiver, the frightened girl whispered, "Nancy, please stay."

The young detective waited. Mr. Everett's voice was very mild. "Hello, Marilyn dear. I'm so sorry I've worried you. Please forgive me. I want to explain everything to you and take back some of my words that I'm afraid you misunderstood. I wouldn't do a thing to hurt your father's memory, or you. I'm asking a favor. Will you please meet me at the amusement park tomorrow morning at nine o'clock? I'll see that the entrance gate is unlocked."

Nancy, who had her ear right next to the phone, heard all this and was troubled. She felt only distrust of Roscoe, but knew that he should be given a chance to either square himself or be found guilty of forgery for certain.

"Hello, Marilyn. Are you still there?" he said.

"Yes. I'm thinking." She glanced toward Nancy, who nodded. "All right. Nine o'clock."

"Great!" her uncle said. "I'll meet you in front of the Crystal Maze. Good-bye for now." He hung up.

"Oh, I'm so frightened," Marilyn said.

"I don't blame you," Nancy replied. "But Frank, Joe, and I will be nearby to guard you."

The girls told the plan to Mr. Drew and Hannah Gruen. The lawyer frowned and said, "Be very careful that man doesn't trick you. Watch your step!"

Hannah Gruen said, "Don't be too easy on him," then added gently, "Why don't we four go to see the show at the park tonight and get another glimpse of the fantastic pyramid?"

Nancy and her father thought this would be a good way to distract Marilyn from her worries, and agreed to go.

When the Bayport gym team came on stage, there was loud applause. The visiting performers had already received high praise from the local community. The pyramid formation was preceded by a series of tumbling acts. The boys did handsprings, then somersaults singly and in pairs so fast that Hannah declared she was becoming dizzy.

"They're really very good," Mr. Drew commented, as the boys took their positions for forming the pyramid. Quickly, they made the climb and stood poised a few moments. As they were about to perform the more difficult position, a pole with a padded tip was rammed from high up backstage, directly between Joe's shoulders.

"Oh!" he exclaimed and lost his balance.

He fell against the boys below him, but managed to jump to the floor. The whole pyramid collapsed as the performers toppled over, sprawling flat. Many people in the audience had jumped to their feet in shock and worry.

Nancy and her father had seen the pole strike Joe and now hurried backstage to locate the culprit. The only person they found was a stagehand who was lying on the floor just regaining consciousness. He revealed having been knocked out by a big fellow with a pole. "I never saw him before."

The hunt for the man proved fruitless. Nancy felt sure he was Roscoe Everett's confederate, and wondered if Marilyn should cancel her morning appointment. It was evident that her uncle was determined to keep the three sleuths from interfering with his plans.

Meanwhile, the pyramiders reassembled and

completed their performances, receiving thunderous applause.

When Nancy and her friends gathered at the Drew home, they talked over the evening's near-tragedy. All of them were worried and wondered how to proceed.

"It's too dangerous," Marilyn declared. "I can't let you continue working on the case."

"If we don't," said Joe, "you may be penniless." Then he grinned. "You don't think we're going to stand by and let you be robbed, do you?"

Marilyn was forced to smile. "I can't tell you how much I appreciate all of your help. Thank you."

The following morning, Mr. Drew dropped Marilyn off at the amusement park gate, then drove on to his office. Nancy followed in her car to the amusement park but hid in a clump of trees just outside the gate. Frank and Joe parked a block away and joined Nancy.

Marilyn had let herself inside the park and walked to the Crystal Maze. In a few minutes, she was joined by her Uncle Roscoe. They talked a few minutes, then went inside the building.

"I don't like this," Nancy whispered to Frank and Joe.

"Neither do I," Joe said. "Let's follow them."

As he started off, Frank put a restraining hand on him. "Why not split up?" he suggested. "We should watch the entrance and also the back of the building."

"I'll go inside," Nancy offered. "If I'm not back in ten minutes, you come in and find me."

The boys agreed and Nancy went ahead. No one else was at the park, since it would not open for another hour. Apparently, Uncle Roscoe had unlocked the front gate himself in anticipation of his morning guest.

As Nancy entered the maze, Frank watched the entrance and exit openings in the lobby while Joe hurried to the rear of the structure. He paused near the tiny hole, which Nancy suspected might be a keyhole.

Meanwhile, Nancy, walking quietly, advanced along the mirrored corridor. No one was in sight. Suddenly, she saw a man advancing towards her, a threatening look on his face. It was impossible, because of the mirrors, to know just how close he was. She started to run, but found herself bumping into the mirror in front of her.

"You'll never get away, Miss Nancy Drew, I've got you now!" said the big man. He began to move quickly, but was also thwarted by the tricky maze.

Nancy was careful not to make a sound that would give the man a clue to her position in the maze. She was terrified, but made herself move slowly and carefully, inching herself along the wall. She turned a corner and lost sight of the burly man. She hoped that he would lose patience and leave the maze, or that she would find her friend before the man found her.

Suddenly, she heard muffled voices from behind one wall. She put her ear to a point where two of the glass panels came together.

At first faintly, then more clearly, she heard Marilyn say, "I won't sign! I'll never sign!"

A man's voice replied, "You'll sign now that this is your father's handwriting or stay here until you do!"

"It's similar, but I'm sure that's not my father's writing!" Marilyn exclaimed. "It's a forgery!"

This was enough for Nancy. Roscoe Everett had played his hand. She must rescue her friend. The girl detective pounded on one of the panels until her hand stung. To her amazement, it began to open. A door! The interlocking bolts on one side reminded Nancy of a door to a bank vault.

For a few seconds, she debated about stepping inside the tiny room beyond. Then came a cry from behind another door. "Let go of my

103

hand! You can't make me sign! Help! Help!"

Nancy made up her mind quickly. She yanked the scarf from her neck and laid it on the sill, so it was half in and half out of the room. Then she stepped inside and the heavy glass door swung shut. Nancy's heart was pounding.

Just then the inner door opened. A man stood there, a satisfied smirk on his face.

"How do you do, Miss Drew, famous amateur detective. You've been giving my niece very bad advice. The only way you'll solve this mystery is to witness Marilyn's signature."

"But I haven't signed anything," Marilyn cried out.

"Good," Nancy said.

Roscoe Everett's eyes gleamed irately. "She's just being stubborn, but she'll sign. And you, Miss Detective, will sign as a witness.

"What do the letters say?" Nancy asked, glancing at several lying on the desk where Marilyn was seated.

"They prove," the man replied, "that Marilyn's father borrowed a lot of money from me and never paid it back."

Marilyn cried out, "Don't believe him, Nancy. He forged the letters on the stolen stationery."

Her uncle suddenly glared at the two girls,

then roared at Marilyn, "You're not going to defy me any more! Sign fast, both of you, or you'll never leave this place, and no one will ever find you!"

As he stopped speaking, Nancy could detect tapping sounds and realized it was a code message: KEEP TALKING. She concluded that it was a message from Frank and Joe, who must have followed her. They had found her scarf!

In a very loud voice, she said, "Mr. Everett, please calm down. Before I sign these papers, I want to know exactly what I'm signing."

"It's none of your business!" he shouted.

Meanwhile, out in the mirrored corridor, Frank and Joe were working feverishly to gain entrance to the man's office.

"I'll run around to the rear and see what I can find out," Joe offered.

Frank said, "On your way back, get our tool kit from the car."

His brother was not gone long. As he rounded the corner of the building, he saw the big man they suspected was Everett's bodyguard, burglar, and roller-coaster culprit, stationed in front of the small hole in the wall.

No chance to get past that hulk, Joe told himself, and raced the other way to get the tool kit.

There were no phones nearby for him to call the police, and the one in the boys' car was being repaired. He and his brother had to make the rescue themselves.

When he rejoined Frank, the argument and threats inside the office were still going on. The boys took slim files out of the tool kit and inserted them in the barely perceptible crack of the door which Nancy's scarf had indicated. But they could make no progress on the lock.

"Interlocking, like our pyramid," said Frank. "Let's try the next one. That may be less complicated."

This time they had better luck. The files indicated that the glass sections were hooked together, not interlocked. Giving the files added leverage with thrusts of covered, noiseless hammers, the boys managed to unfasten the whole series of large steel hooks. The panel, attached to a wooden frame, swung out easily.

Frank and Joe stepped behind it. A thin beaverboard wall separated the space from the office. Frank found a hole and pulled part of the wall apart. The boys stared in amazement. Nancy and Marilyn were on the floor, bound and gagged. Roscoe Everett and his bodyguard were just about to leave by a rear door.

The brothers jumped on them and a tussle

ensued. The Hardys subdued Uncle Roscoe easily, but were no match for the big man. They might have lost the fight, but suddenly through the opening from the corridor rushed Mr. Drew and two police officers. They revealed that the big man was wanted on burglary charges. The police handcuffed him.

Uncle Roscoe's bravado was gone. As Frank and Joe released the girls, he confessed to Mr. Drew that his whole story about Marilyn's father owing him money was false, and he had indeed forged the letters he planned to use.

"But this maze belongs to me!" he cried out. "I invented the interlocking mirrors and thought no one could ever find my office. I thought I could hide here forever!"

Nancy asked, "How did you open the door for me to come in?"

Roscoe Everett pointed to a button on the wall near his desk.

Mr. Drew said, "Marilyn, do you want to place charges against your uncle?"

The girl thought a moment, then said, "Not to go to prison. I think he should be placed in a hospital for treatment and a long rest."

As the two officers led him away, Marilyn suddenly hugged Mr. Drew and the three young sleuths.

"You are just the most wonderful friends anybody could ever have!" she declared. "Frank and Joe are not only interlocking pyramiders, but interlocking sleuths as well. And Nancy, you are amazing!"

THE BANK ROBBERY PUZZLE

"I can't believe it!" Frank Hardy called out. He was reading part of the *Bayport Times*. As his brother Joe and Nancy Drew looked over at him, he continued, "The rash of bank robberies in this area is getting worse! They're happening all over the county!"

The other two stared at him, surprised. Nancy, who had arrived only the day before to visit the Hardys, asked, "Is there something new in the paper?"

Frank showed her an article on the front page. "It just says that Harpersville was recently hit, and the robbers got away without leaving a clue," he explained.

As Nancy began to read the column, Joe suddenly exclaimed, "Look at this!" He was staring at a crossword puzzle in the paper on which he had been working. "I wonder if this has anything to do with the robberies."

Looking over Joe's shoulder, Frank asked, "What exactly are you talking about?"

"Look at this crossword puzzle," Joe answered excitedly. "These words across seem to form a message." He continued to work on the puzzle for a few minutes, while Frank and Nancy waited curiously. Moments later, Joe looked up and said, "I think there's something to this." He pointed to the words which, when read together, said: MEET AT BANK. WEAR RED TIE.

"But how can you be so sure there's a connection between the crossword and the robberies?" Nancy asked.

Joe explained that the authorities had been unable to determine how the thieves communicated with one another. The ring of criminals was reportedly rather large, but the police hadn't been able to find any letters, identify any signals, or tap any phone calls among the criminals.

"This could be the way they communicate. Through the local newspaper!" Nancy exclaimed.

"If our hunch is right," Frank added, "these could be instructions for a robbery at the Bayport Bank!"

"Wow!" Joe said. "If we're right, we should do something about it right away."

Nancy suggested that they look very carefully for other clues in the crossword to see if there might be another message.

She and Joe leaned over Frank's shoulder and looked at each word. Suddenly, Frank put his finger on one and exclaimed, "Opening!" He thought for a moment. "That could be when they're supposed to meet. But it couldn't mean today—this is the afternoon edition of the paper."

"But it could mean tomorrow," Joe said. "We'd better look into this."

The other two young sleuths agreed, but debated about the best way to proceed. Frank said, "I'm sure Police Chief Collig would be interested."

Nancy nodded, but added, "First, though, we should find out more about this puzzle. All it says here is that it's submitted by 'A Reader.' If we could find out who the author is, the puzzle might be easily explained."

Frank and Joe agreed and suggested that they go at once to the office of the *Bayport Times*.

When they arrived, Frank asked to see the manager, Mr. Watkin, whom the boys knew well. He welcomed them with a smile. "Don't tell me you've brought a mystery for our paper to print!"

"Maybe." Joe smiled back. He then asked Mr. Watkin if he knew anything about the author of that afternoon's crossword puzzle.

"Not much," Mr. Watkin replied. "We frequently accept puzzles from our readers. We don't pay for them, so as long as the puzzle works, we publish it."

"Did you meet this particular author?" Nancy asked hopefully.

"Yes, I did. He was an elderly man—said it was composed by his grandson and wanted it published today because it was his grandson's birthday and he thought it would be a nice surprise."

"Can you describe him?" Joe inquired. "And did he give his name?"

"Well, he was nice-looking—had gray hair and was a bit stout. I don't remember his name, or even if he gave one."

"Thank you so much. You've been a great help," Joe said, shaking Mr. Watkin's hand. The three young detectives left the newspaper office and discussed their findings.

"I think it's time we talk to Chief Collig," Frank urged.

After hearing their theory, the head of the

Bayport police force frowned, then said, "It sounds a little bit farfetched to me, but I'll give it a try."

He told them he would assign plainclothes-men to the bank. "They can go in one by one when the doors open tomorrow morning. If you young folks are correct, the thieves should be right on their heels."

Joe asked, "Where do *we* fit into the picture?"

Chief Collig smiled tolerantly. "You can hear about the robbery on the newscast."

"But we want to be in on the action," Joe persisted.

The chief thought for a moment. Finally, he said, "How would it be if you two boys go in before the bank is officially open? You can hide in one of the small rooms where people take their safe-deposit boxes to look at the contents. We'll give you a walkie-talkie so you can contact the plainclothesmen should you spot any trouble. I'll arrange everything with the bank."

Frank and Joe were delighted with the plan, but Nancy's heart sank. She knew Chief Collig would never allow her to be exposed to any danger.

Finally, she smiled at him and said, "I have a wonderful high-speed camera. Would you let me stay outside and try to get pictures of any customers wearing red ties?"

The chief said he thought this would be safe enough as long as she did not stand too close to the bank entrance. Then another idea came into her mind. She said, "I could wear a disguise in case the robbers recognize me. I'll dress like an old woman with a basket of flowers and try to sell them. I'll give the proceeds to the Bayport Children's Hospital."

The chief liked her idea. He suggested, however, that she have someone with her. "How about one of your pals? She could help sell flowers while you snap pictures."

The plan was set and the three sleuths hurried to the Hardy home to tell the others. It took some persuasion to talk Mrs. Hardy into agreeing, but she finally did so on their promise to be extremely careful in their eavesdropping.

Aunt Gertrude was more vociferous. "Suppose the robbers are big, burly brutes. They could make Three-Sleuth Stew out of you!"

Everyone laughed, and Frank reassured her by saying that, from the newspaper accounts of other bank robberies in the area, the men had gone about their business quickly and harmed no one.

Nancy told her plan and asked the women if

they had any clothes that would fit her, and by any chance, a gray wig. Mrs. Hardy replied, "I have just the costume. I was in a play last year at the women's club and wore an ankle-length black dress and a gray wig. Come upstairs and try them on."

A short time later, as a transformed Nancy was descending the steps, Mr. Hardy walked in the front door. He stopped short and apparently did not recognize the girl for a moment. In a high-pitched voice she said, "Good evening, Mr. Hardy. I hope you don't mind one extra to dinner." Then she came down the steps and gave him a hug.

Suddenly, he burst into laughter. "Nancy—is that you? What a good disguise! Where are you going to wear it?"

When she told him, his forehead wrinkled. "Did Chief Collig give you permission to do this?"

"Yes, and the boys will tell you what they're going to do. We want to help foil the bank robbers, perhaps tomorrow morning."

When he heard Frank and Joe's plan, their father looked stern and said, "You guys better be careful. Now tell me the whole story—slowly."

After hearing it, he congratulated the three

sleuths for their quick thinking, but warned them not to be disappointed if the robbers wearing red ties never showed up.

Frank grinned. "To tell the truth, Dad, we hope they don't!"

Nancy's first move was to drive downtown to a florist's shop and purchase a large basket and several dozen bright-colored carnations.

The following morning everyone in the house was up early. Mrs. Hardy declared that she felt jittery about the venture, but did not ask the young people to change their minds.

Since Mr. Hardy was well-known in town and probably to the bank robbers, he left alone and drove directly to his office. Nancy went off next in her own car and picked up Bess Marvin, a pretty, slightly plump girl who was one of Nancy's closest friends. Bess, who was also visiting in Bayport, had worked on many cases with Nancy.

Frank and Joe went off in their own car and were admitted by a guard at the rear entrance to the bank. They hurried at once to the safe-deposit booth nearest the main room.

Though the glass door was opaque, they kept the door open a crack to peer out. Should there be any trouble, they would immediately call the police.

Soon, officers and tellers began to arrive. When everyone was at his or her post, a guard opened the door of the great vault, which had been automatically unlocked by a timer.

Outside the building, Nancy and Bess had taken positions a few feet from the entrance. Nancy was seated in a chair, wearing her disguise, her camera hidden under the folds of her dress. Bess was winning customers with her dimpled smile. A group had gathered by now, waiting for the bank to open.

Nancy's keen eyes were roving over the group. She spotted a man wearing a red necktie coming toward the entrance. Without his being aware of it, she photographed him several times. A little behind him was another man, also wearing a red necktie. The young detective waited until he was not looking in the girls' direction, then snapped high-speed pictures of him. Both men were of medium height and build, and had dark hair.

Nancy also noted that the two men had arrived in a car which was now parked at the curb. The driver sat at the wheel with the motor running.

The getaway car, she thought. "I must get the driver's picture," she told Bess. "Distract him by offering him some flowers."

The scheme worked well and both girls returned to their spot near the entrance.

Meanwhile, Frank and Joe were watching the scene in the bank. The two men with red neckties had gone to different tellers. Frank and Joe could not hear what was said, but noted that two other customers, who they believed were plainclothesmen, closed in behind the suspects. As large sums of money were handed out to them, the robbers were nabbed by the police. Both men put up a fierce fight and tried to get away, but bank guards, alerted by Frank and Joe, quickly came to subdue them. Protesting, the thieves were handcuffed and led from the building.

"Pretty smooth capture," Frank remarked, then said, "But look!"

The Hardys were about to leave their booth when they saw two men holding a safe-deposit box go into the adjoining booth and lock the door. Both wore red-and-white striped shirts. Frank and Joe watched the booth carefully.

Frank pulled an electronic listening device from his pocket. He stuck it against the wall to the adjoining booth, hoping it would pick up revealing information. Meanwhile, Joe planted a tiny tape recorder just below the bug.

The boys did not have long to wait. Although

the men talked in whispers, their conversation came across clearly. They were taking a lot of money from their pockets and putting it in the box, which already contained a large quantity of currency. Their conversation indicated that they were in a hurry to get away, and one said, "We don't want to be wiped out like the others!"

Frank and Joe hestitated no longer. They put their recording equipment into their pockets and quickly spoke into their walkie-talkie to alert one of the bank guards. Within seconds, four plainclothesmen took charge of the two suspects with their safe-deposit box in hand.

The men protested loudly but Frank and Joe explained what they had heard from the next booth. The prisoners were taken completely by surprise. Hurling threats at the Hardys, they were taken away. The bank president, Mr. Blake, congratulated Frank and Joe on their fine work. He added, "I hope this stops these terrible robberies!"

Frank said, "I'm afraid I have a strong suspicion that there are other thieves still at large—including the ringleader. I saw no one that fit the description of the man who brought in the crossword puzzle to the newspaper."

The boys walked outside. Nancy and Bess

were displaying their few remaining flowers.

"Success, eh?" Frank remarked.

"Yes," Bess replied. "But thank goodness it's over. I was terrified the whole time. I'm glad you boys are okay. Guess what? Nancy snapped pictures of the red-tie men and the driver of the getaway car!"

Nancy added, "The car made a speedy exit when the driver saw his pals coming out handcuffed."

She drove Bess to her friend's home, then joined Frank and Joe at police headquarters. The boys were telling what they had overheard and had given the incriminating tape to Chief Collig.

When they finished, Frank asked, "Chief, will you write down the names of all the banks in our area that have been robbed?"

The officer did so, then said, "I presume this means you're going to continue working on the case."

"You bet," said Joe with a grin. "By the way, Chief Collig, do all the towns that have been hit by robberies have their own newspapers?"

After thinking for a moment, the officer replied, "Well, I can't be sure, but I believe they do."

As soon as the three sleuths were outdoors,

Frank looked at the list and said, "Why don't we go over to Harpersville and look at back issues of the paper? Maybe we can pick up a clue."

"Good idea," Nancy said.

They went at once to the newspaper office in Harpersville and asked to look through its files. After reading one article about the recent bank robbery, the sleuths began looking in the previous publications.

Nancy chose one that had been published the day before the robbery. As she looked through it column by column, she came to the crossword puzzle.

"I'm going to work this out!" she whispered. "This was also submitted by 'A Reader.' Let's see if there's anything here."

Frank and Joe came to her side as she began filling in the clues for the words across. Nothing appeared. Disappointed, Nancy was about to close the paper when Joe had an idea.

"Try the downs, Nancy," he suggested.

Quickly, she finished the puzzle and, as the sleuths suspected, a message appeared: MEET AT BANK. WEAR GREEN TIE.

"Super!" Joe exclaimed. "Now that we have a description of the man, perhaps we can meet someone else who saw him. We could try the local inn here first. The robbers had to stay somewhere."

Upon reaching the inn a few minutes later, Frank approached the desk clerk and gave him the description they had received from Mr. Watkin.

The clerk, named Mr. Clifford, thought for a moment. "Yes, I do believe I remember him. His name is Sidney Andrews. But he left here three days ago."

The three sleuths looked at one another. That was the day of the Harpersville robbery!

Frank thanked him for the information. As the three callers approached the outer door, an elderly woman, who was very pale, came in. She clutched Nancy's arm and said, "My dear, I feel very ill. Would you please help me to the ladies' restroom?"

"I'll be glad to," Nancy replied, taking the woman's arm.

Frank and Joe told Nancy they would sit down and wait for her. She and the stranger disappeared around a corner.

"I'll just bet that Sidney Andrews is the mastermind of the bank robbery gang!" Frank declared.

"I think so too," his brother replied, and looked at his wristwatch. "Nancy's been gone a long time. If that woman is ill, we should call a doctor."

"Nancy's probably giving her first aid," Frank suggested.

When another fifteen minutes went by and Nancy had not reappeared, Frank and Joe began to worry that something was really wrong. They spoke to Mr. Clifford, who in turn went for Mr. Smith, the manager. Mr. Smith and the two boys hurried to the ladies' restroom and knocked. There was no answer.

Frank called loudly into the crack of the door, "Nancy!"

Still there was no reply, so Mr. Smith opened the door. Stretched on the floor, unconscious, was Nancy Drew! The elderly woman had vanished.

"How dreadful!" the manager exclaimed. "I'll phone for an ambulance."

"Just a minute!" Frank said. "I think Nancy is regaining consciousness."

In a few seconds, the girl opened her eyes, blinked, then closed them again. Frank and Joe fanned the air near her face and presently she opened her eyes again.

"You found me!" she whispered.

Mr. Smith advised her not to sit up right away and Joe asked her what had happened.

"That woman—she must be part of the robbery gang. Right after we walked in here, she said, 'Nancy Drew, you and your friends shouldn't be so nosy . . . I'll fix you!' She opened her handbag and the next instant held something under my nose and I blacked out immediately."

As Mr. Smith and the boys helped Nancy to her feet, the manager asked what the woman had meant and why she wanted to injure the girl.

"We're amateur detectives," Frank explained. "All of us are trying to track down the bank robbers who have been working in this county. Some of them have been put in jail, but evidently this is a large gang. Incidentally, the guest you had here who called himself Sidney Andrews is probably the leader. Have you any idea where he went after he left here?"

"No," Mr. Smith replied. "And would you mind telling me who you are?"

The three revealed their identities and at once the manager said, "Hardy? Are you related to the detective Fenton Hardy?"

"We're his sons," Joe answered. "And Nancy Drew is a well-known amateur detective, too."

The man's eyebrows shot up. "I've read about you in the newspapers," he said. "You're very adventuresome!"

Nancy soon recovered fully, and suggested they all go home and sort out the information they had uncovered that afternoon. On the way, Frank remarked to Nancy, "I guess Joe and I had better not let you out of our sight!"

Just then, Nancy put her hand into one of her dress pockets. Feeling a paper inside, she pulled it out.

"Listen to this!" she said. "A note from that 'sweet' old lady. It says: CALL OFF YOUR HOUNDS OR YOU'LL REGRET IT."

"I don't like this one bit," Joe said grimly. "I think Chief Collig should be notified."

When they told the chief their story, he was amazed and said, "To think that you could escape being harmed at a bank holdup, and then be conned by a pleasant old woman. Nancy, I'm sorry about this, and I'm glad you weren't hurt badly."

The following day the three sleuths headed for Franklin, and went at once to the library to look for the town newspaper. To their chagrin, they were not allowed to look through the files. Mr. Fisher, the librarian, was adamant.

"We were warned against letting in three teenagers—two boys and a girl."

"I think we can explain." Frank said and pulled out an identification card. Joe and Nancy did also.

Mr. Fisher reddened. "So you're the Hardy boys and Nancy Drew," he said. "Well, why didn't you *say* so? Go ahead and look through our files."

The young people thanked him and said that they suspected someone connected with the band of robbers had tried to delay their sleuthing.

A young office assistant led them to the files. Soon they were hunting for the edition of the paper published the day before the local bank robbery.

The search took just a few moments. Nancy came upon the crossword puzzle that was composed by "A Reader." Intrigued, Nancy, Frank, and Joe began to work it out.

"The puzzlemaker is at it again!" Nancy exclaimed. "Look at this message! MEET AT BANK. WEAR GOLD TIE."

"Pretty clever," Joe remarked.

"What puzzles me," Frank said, "is why the puzzlemaker uses newspapers to give messages to his men instead of having private meetings."

"Probably," said Nancy, "he doesn't want them to know who he is."

Frank said he would suggest to Chief Collig that every newspaper in the county be warned not to take any crosswords from people they didn't know until the mystery was solved. They then packed up their gear and headed for home.

All of the time that Frank had been driving, Joe had been periodically looking out the rear window. Suddenly, he said, "I think we're being followed." In response, Frank put on a burst of speed.

So did the other driver. Frank dropped back to the normal speed limit. A few seconds later, the car behind suddenly passed them in a rush. In moments, it met a sedan coming from the opposite direction. The drivers saluted, then went on.

Seconds afterward, the driver of the oncoming car stopped abruptly, opened the door, and jumped out. He took a huge bucket from the seat and just before Frank reached the spot, threw the contents onto the road. Then he jumped into his car and whizzed backward.

"Oil!" Joe cried out.

Frank jammed on the brakes, but was too late. The car ran onto the oil, swung in a circle, then landed on its side in a ditch!

"Oh!" moaned Joe, whose head had hit a window.

Nancy and Frank were shaken up, but not hurt. Fortunately, the car had landed in a soft, muddy ditch instead of on cement. Nancy and Joe climbed out of the car, shook themselves, and walked around to collect their wits. Meanwhile, Frank had picked up the car's telephone and phoned Bayport police headquarters.

Chief Collig was astounded at Frank's story and said he would send a wrecker, the First Aid Squad, and a sander immediately. "And I'll see that the road is closed off at once! Exactly where are you?"

Frank told him and then hung up. In a short while, the First Aid Squad appeared. One of the men examined the three victims to check for any serious injuries.

"Guess you're okay," he said. "You three are mighty lucky to have come out of this so well. What happened?"

Frank told the story and the three rescue workers shook their heads. "I hope they nab those fools," one of them said, as he gave Joe an ice bag for the side of his face.

A police car from the local area arrived, together with a wrecker. The driver looked at the mess on the road and said it would be a tough job to move the Hardy car away from the oil and out of the ditch. It took the workmen nearly an hour.

In the meantime, the police had set up roadblocks since the sander had not arrived. When the car was finally on the road, Frank got in, afraid it would not start. But the engine caught!

"Hurray!" he cried out, then drove the sedan down the road to be sure the wheels and brakes were working properly. Satisfied, he backed up and told Nancy and Joe to climb in.

"Oh, I just remembered something," the girl detective said to the police. "I have the license numbers of the two cars responsible for our accident."

The police wrote them down, then the young detectives rode off. Upon their arrival home, Mrs. Hardy and Aunt Gertrude exclaimed about the young people's messed-up hair and clothes. "Whatever happened to you?" the boys' mother asked, seeing the bruise on Joe's cheek.

Joe told the story. When he finished, Aunt Gertrude exclaimed, "How wicked of that man with the bucket!"

"I agree," said Joe.

Mrs. Hardy looked fondly at the three young people. "I'm so thankful the accident was no worse. You know, sometimes I wish you would all give up this detective business. It's too dangerous!

At this point in the discussion Mr. Hardy's assistant, Sam Radley, walked in. He, too, was amazed at what had happened. "And here I am bringing you newspapers from all over the county which'll probably get you into *more* trouble!"

The three teenagers laughed, and Nancy said, "If there's a clue to this mystery in them, let's have them!"

Sam was a great favorite with the three young sleuths and loved to talk to them, but now he was in a hurry to get home so he did not stay long. As soon as he left, Nancy, Frank, and Joe began to read the papers.

After twenty minutes had gone by, Aunt Gertrude remarked to Mrs. Hardy, "Laura, I haven't heard this house so quiet in years!"

Her sister-in-law nodded. "They haven't found anything exciting, I guess, or they would have shouted."

It was true. Nancy, Frank, and Joe had looked through many of the newspapers only to find that the crosswords in those papers were syndicated and by well-known authors.

Finally, Nancy found one in *The Littleton Press* with "A Reader" given as the author and quickly worked it out. "Here's another clue! It says DINNER ... RIVERSIDE ... THURSDAY ... FRIENDLY EIGHT ... SEVEN ... BLUE ... TIES. What could that mean?"

"Well, there's a restaurant in Littleton called The Riverside. It sounds as if a meeting is being set up. I guess the gang's name is the Friendly Eight."

They decided to be there when the gang met. "Today's Thursday. Why don't I make a reservation at The Riverside?" Joe encouraged.

"Why not include your whole family?" Nancy suggested. "Then it will look more like a party and not obvious spying."

Joe agreed, but said, "Don't forget that some of the bank robbers know us though we don't know them."

Frank sighed. "Let's call Dad and get his opinion."

The detective first asked what had happened to the young sleuths that day and praised their work. "It's too bad you had to find out the hard way who some of those crooks are. I think your idea for the stakeout in the restaurant is a good one. When you call the restaurant for a reservation, find out exactly where it's located."

Frank made a reservation for the whole family and Nancy, and with great interest learned that the restaurant was next to the Littleton Bank.

When Mr. Hardy came home, he told the others that he had a report on the two cars which had been involved in the oil slick.

"One of the cars had been stolen and the other had stolen license plates on it."

"Then there's not much chance of identifying the drivers," Nancy remarked.

"I'm afraid not," Mr. Hardy agreed, "but the police are working on it."

The group then freshened up and left for the restaurant. As they rode up to it, Joe remarked, "It's sure close to the bank. Barely air space between the buildings."

The Hardys and Nancy took their seats and picked up the menu cards.

They glanced around the room. Nancy suddenly gasped. "That's the man who was driving the getaway car! The others at the table must be members of the gang. There are eight places set, but there are only six there. I wonder where the other two members of the Friendly Eight are."

Both the Hardy group and the suspects gave their orders to waiters. There was no conversation at the gang's table, but Nancy studied the men intently. She was sure that a rather stout, gray-haired man was the author of the crossword puzzles. There were only six men at the table. Nancy wondered if there were others still coming.

As the group of suspects finished the main course, one of the men got up. Without saying a word, he went into the kitchen. Nancy and the Hardys looked at one another. Minutes later another man followed.

"I think it's time for us to make a move," Frank whispered. "I'll try a ruse." He stood up and pretended to waver as if he were dizzy. Aloud, he said, "I feel faint. Somebody help me to the back door so I can get fresh air."

Joe jumped up, put an arm around Frank, and helped him into the kitchen. The boys spotted the back door, but decided to try another one. Joe yanked it open. Steps led to the basement.

Instantly, a chef standing nearby dashed over and said, "Nobody can go down there! Repairmen are at work." He slammed the door.

"Where's the-the back door?" Frank asked faintly.

The chef pointed. "And don't come back!"

The Hardys made it to the door while the other workers followed them with their eyes. When the brothers reached the alleyway, Frank said in a loud voice, "I feel better. Let's go back inside."

"Take it easy!" Joe advised in an even louder tone. "It might have been your heart!"

The boys made it to the front door and went

inside. Frank declared he felt all right now, but instead of returning to their table, the brothers went to the office of the manager, Mr. Phillip.

Joe closed the door and the boys introduced themselves. Frank said, "We're sorry to bother you, but we'd like you to answer a question. We think two customers are in your basement."

"Who let them down there?" the manager asked.

"We don't know, but when my brother and I walked into the kitchen trying to get to the back door, the head chef yelled that we couldn't go to the basement because repairmen are at work."

"That's not true," Mr. Phillip said. "I'll look into this at once."

Joe spoke up. "I wouldn't advise that. To tell you the truth, we think those men are anything but friendly. We suspect they're bank robbers!"

"What!" the manager cried out.

"You'd better notify the police instead," Frank warned. "Those repairmen may be breaking into the bank. Joe and I will go back to our table and watch what's going on."

"Well, thank you," Mr. Phillip said. "I'll call the police right now and tell them what you said." He picked up the telephone and dialed.

The boys waited to be sure he reached the police, then went back to their table.

"Do you feel better?" Mrs. Hardy asked Frank.

"Oh, yes," her son replied. "All I needed was some fresh air."

A few minutes later, two men wearing small health-inspector badges walked into the restaurant. They spoke to the manager, then came directly toward the rear where the Hardys were seated.

"Hello," one of them said.

"Why, how do you do?" Mr. Hardy responded casually. "You here to inspect?"

The men nodded to Mr. Hardy, then went directly into the kitchen. The detective explained to his family that he knew the two men, who were policemen posing as food inspectors.

Mr. Hardy decided to play a little game. He said in a loud voice, "The chicken I ordered is terrible. I think it may be bad. I didn't want to say anything to the waiter, but Frank and Joe, why don't you go tell those food inspectors?"

The two boys rose from the table and went into the kitchen to watch the "inspectors." The two men had stopped to speak to the head chef and chief suspect, who was very obliging in his answers and praised the cleanliness and good food. The two investigators went from counter to counter and looked into simmering pots on the immense stove.

"Things look okay," Rick, one of the investigators, said, and moved toward the door to the basement, "but I think we'd better take a look downstairs."

At once, the head chef left his station and guarded the door. "You can't go down there!" he said.

"Why not?" Rick asked.

"Because this is private property," he snarled.

Frank and Joe moved closer. If there was to be a struggle, maybe they could hold back the chef while the two policemen went to the basement.

"Stand aside! Get out of here!" the chef yelled.

The altercation brought other kitchen workers to the scene. As the two policemen shoved the chef aside, Frank and Joe moved in and held the man's arms behind him. Irate, he began to kick them. A cook and a waiter pinned the man's legs.

"Get out! Get out of my way!" the chef kept on.

In the meantime, the two policemen opened the door to the basement and raced down the stairs. Frank and Joe warned the men holding the chef not to let him go. "He's a suspect!" Joe cried out.

The boys followed the policemen down the stairway.

By now, the officers had reached an opening in a side wall from which bricks had been re-moved. Just outside was an opening into the basement of the bank!

Rick turned and whispered to the boys, "Don't follow us. Those men are probably armed."

The officers stepped through the opening. As they advanced, Frank and Joe could see two dark-haired men with beards and mustaches on a stepladder drilling a hole through the floor of the bank!

Frank and Joe wondered what they should do. Frank whispered, "You stay here and watch, but keep out of sight. I'll go for the police."

He ran back through the restaurant opening and hurried up the stairway to the kitchen. The room was full of people, but the head chef was gone. Frank asked where he was.

The cook said, "He tried to escape into the alley, but a policeman out there stopped him."

Frank sped into the alleyway. Two officers stood there guarding the kitchen door. Quickly,

Frank told them what was going on in the basement of the bank and offered to show them the way. By the time they reached the spot, the two "food inspectors" had nabbed the robbers.

Taken off guard, the suspects had no time to use any firearms. They put up a fight, but with the strength of the two extra officers, they were soon subdued. They were handcuffed and led back through the basement and up the stairs to the kitchen.

Frank hurried into the restaurant to his family's table. Only Mrs. Hardy and his aunt were there.

"Where are the others?" Frank asked.

"Up front," Aunt Gertrude replied. "Nancy went to alert the police about the gang and your father followed them when they left their places."

"Oh, I hope everyone's all right," said Mrs. Hardy.

Joe arrived in a few minutes. He and Frank went to the front of the restaurant. In the manager's office were the man suspected of being the puzzlemaker, the driver of the getaway car, Nancy, Mr. Hardy, the manager, and four police officers.

The gray-haired puzzlemaker was declaring his innocence and saying he had no connection with the robbers. No one believed him, but when he was confronted with the clues that had led to his arrest, the man confessed and bragged about how smart he was. "Nobody can make better puzzles than I," he boasted as the others looked on. Asked about the Friendly Eight, he said, "I'm the mastermind, and there are many who obey my commands, but these seven are my closest associates. Personally, I've never robbed a bank, or been inside one when my men were at work."

He was handcuffed and led away with the driver, whom Nancy now identified. Another officer came inside with a report. He had been communicating by his car phone with police headquarters. Now he asked, "Are you Nancy Drew and the Hardy boys?"

"Yes, we are," the three chorused.

"Our police chief just had a message from your Chief Collig. The men responsible for your auto accident have been captured. We think now the bank robbery case is all wrapped up. And your 'old lady' attacker, Nancy, was another gang member in disguise. We caught him as well. His job was to stick around in each town a few days after the robberies occurred and make sure the gang's tracks were covered. But now it looks as if we've got them all."

"Thank goodness for that!" the restaurant manager burst out, quite upset by the whole incident.

A cheer went up from the group. By this time, Mrs. Hardy and Aunt Gertrude had joined the others in the kitchen. When they heard the news, they, too, gave a cheer.

"And now, let's go home." Mrs. Hardy pleaded. "And please . . . no more robbers' puzzles!"

CLUE IN THE CHIMES

The tour bus rattled and creaked as it climbed the steep, rocky road to the hilltop. Nancy, Frank, and Joe were aboard, sitting in the first row.

Ben Nowall, the driver, talked constantly. "You got to forgive Old Betsey—that's what I call this ancient school bus. Been out o' use for kids a long time, but I bought her cheap."

Ben changed the subject. "Good thing you folks ain't superstitious. You know this hillside's got a curse on it. That's right. Nearly a hundred years ago a terrible epidemic broke out among the people living here."

"What kind of epidemic?" Nancy asked.

"I dunno. Nobody ever figured it out," Ben replied, "but folks were dyin' like flies. The rest—men, women, children, little babies—got out in a hurry and never came back. Left everything and went to town."

The passengers looked at the hillside, which was dotted with attractive stone houses. To their amazement, the grass had been cut.

Frank asked, "If no one comes here, who mows the lawns?"

"Fellow from town," Ben answered. "He's not afraid of the outdoors, but you'd never catch him goin' *into* any of those buildings."

Just then, everyone heard the sound of beautiful chimes. Ben stopped the bus, bowed his head, and placed both hands over his ears. He turned white.

"Are you ill?" Nancy said to him.

Ben did not reply until the echoes of the beautiful tones faded away. Then he uncovered his ears and said in an awed voice, "A ghost plays those chimes!"

"Where are they?" Joe asked.

"In the church tower," the driver answered. "We'll be comin' to it soon. But I warn you, that church is haunted. Stay out of it!"

Soon, an ivy-covered, stone building came into view. It stood majestically on the crest of the hill.

As some of the bus passengers got out, Nancy asked if the church was locked.

"Never went close enough to find out," Ben countered.

146

Nancy, Frank, and Joe decided to investigate. Several of the tourists tried to talk them out of it, but the three detectives laughed off the people's fear of a ghost. Frank led the way.

A group of passengers stood admiring the old church. Ben called, "Don't you young folks be long. I got to be gettin' back to town before sunset. Nobody wants to be on this hill in the dark."

"Why not?" Nancy called back.

Ben replied, "Indian ghosts. Go see Grandma Norton. She's kind of an expert on this. She'll tell you all about it."

"Indian ghosts!" Joe repeated. "Let's stay for the show!"

Nancy and Frank laughed, but sobered quickly as the three of them reached the church door and turned the handle. The door creaked open. The vestibule was dark and gloomy, but sunlight streamed into the worship area. Rows of spotless, white-painted pews, long sparkling windows, and a carved-wood chancel amazed the three young sleuths.

"I expected cobwebs and dark shadows!" Frank whispered into the eerie silence.

The others nodded as they walked forward. Two doors opened from the chancel. One was an anteroom for the minister to put on his robe.

In the other room stood a ladder to the tower which held the chimes.

"Let's go up," Nancy suggested eagerly.

One by one, the three climbed and stepped onto the platform above. They gazed in awe at the line of chimes of varying lengths. A huge clapper attached to a bar could be swung so it would hit one chime at a time to play a tune.

Joe lifted the clapper. "I'm a ghost," he said and let it go. *Bong!*

As the clapper returned, Frank grabbed it, swung the bar a trifle, and gave the clapper a push. *Wang!*

"Not very pretty," Nancy commented and took a turn. She chose a short, slender chime. *Ding!* it trilled. In a moment, she added, "We'd better go back or the bus will leave without us."

Frank walked to the opening and cried out, "The ladder! It's gone!"

"Did it fall down?" Joe asked.

Frank looked to the room below. "No. I don't see it anywhere."

At the top of his lungs, he called through the opening, "Help! Help!" Joe joined him but there was no response.

Nancy dashed to one of the slatted windows, which had wide openings between the shutters. She stared toward the road and the front of the church.

She exclaimed, "The bus has left! Nobody's here!"

Frank was angry. "How could they *do* that to us?"

"Out of fear," Nancy replied. "Remember Ben told us a *ghost* played the chimes. When we hit them, he probably took off in a hurry with the other passengers and figured the ghost got us."

"Looks as if he got the ladder, too!" Joe said. "It couldn't walk away by itself. We could be marooned here for days."

The three frustrated sleuths were silent for a few minutes, then Nancy said, "The ivy. We can climb down the ivy! It looks very strong. I'm sure it would hold us. I weigh the least of the three of us. I'll go first."

"How are you going to get to the ivy?" Joe asked.

"I think I can squeeze between the slats," she replied.

Frank spoke up. "No, Nancy. I'll go first." He wriggled his slim body between the slats, reached for the mass of ivy, and tested its hold.

"Strong as rope," he reported. "Well, here goes!"

The vine proved to be sturdy and so tight to the stonework that only a chisel could pry it loose. Frank reached the ground safely, then

Joe climbed down. Nancy had no trouble following.

"Let's hunt for the ladder," she suggested.

But though they searched inside and outside the church, they could not locate it.

"I'm coming back to find out where it is," Frank declared. "Right now we'd better hurry or we'll miss our bus from town to the dig."

Nancy, Frank, and Joe had joined a student archeological dig a few miles from town. Upon hearing about the haunted hillside, they decided to learn more about it when they had an afternoon off from the dig.

By running the last half-mile, they were able to catch the bus. They arrived at the tented area just as the camp's dinner bell was ringing.

"Sounds good. I'm empty down to my boots," Joe said.

Nancy, grinning, replied, "Are you going to fill them with leftovers for your midnight snack?"

Joe laughed at the jibe.

At the mess table, Professor Thompson, who was in charge of the dig, asked many questions about the haunted hillside. He was intrigued by Nancy's story that Indian ghosts were said to be guarding it.

Students were more interested in the account

of the daring escape from the church tower after the mysterious removal of the ladder.

"I'd still be stuck up there," declared Sue Grandom.

"You probably would," said Bill Fiske, "helping the ghost play the chimes!"

Everyone went to bed early, as work on the dig began at dawn. The following morning Nancy, Frank, and Joe worked together, hoping to uncover an early American Indian relic. Several bones already had been found by the various groups, but no complete skeleton. Today, they were using tiny spades and tweezers to pick up small pieces. When the earth was hard, the workers gently poured water on a spot, then dug in the moist ground.

"Here's a tooth," said Frank. "Maybe the guy had a toothache and had this relic pulled."

Joe took the tooth. "I wonder how old this is."

"Not too old," Nancy guessed, "or it wouldn't be so close to the surface."

"Unless," Frank added, "an earthquake, or a flood, or a volcanic landslide put it here."

The three continued working, getting deeper and deeper into the part of the pit which the young archeologists were making.

There was no conversation until Joe called

out. "Here's something!" He put down his spade and worked carefully with his fingers. In a few minutes, he had uncovered the bones of an ancient arm.

"Let's try to find the rest of the guy," Frank said. "I wonder how old he was when he died."

An hour went by before they had any success. Then Nancy located the skull, which had one tooth missing. The rest was in good condition.

"Which proves," she said, "that this head belonged to a young man, who hadn't been chewing beyond some twenty years."

Other workers and Professor Thompson came to inspect the find. Little by little, more pieces were discovered. The archeologists were excited. They had almost come to locating the relics of a whole human skeleton!

"I believe," said the professor, "that this person died about two hundred years ago!"

"Wow!" Joe exclaimed. "Was he beheaded?"

"We'll know that if we find the backbone."

Digging went on through the afternoon. As each precious part was found, it was carefully wrapped in cotton cloth.

"Here's the man's backbone!" Frank exclaimed. "It's in two parts. Maybe he died of a broken back."

The upper half still held one side of the rib cage. Nancy pointed out a two-inch hole in it. "I think an arrow hit the man," she said.

Professor Thompson confirmed this. He was already busy wiring various pieces together.

When the relic was complete except for one arm, a leg, and the missing half of the man's ribs, Joe held up the skeleton. In a pathetic, choked-up voice, he said, "Please, oh please, find the rest of me. I'm young, I'm handsome. I don't want to be half a man!"

The other diggers laughed and said they would try even harder. They went to work with renewed vigor. Two hours later, students brought their finds to the professor. Nancy presented the missing arm with the fingers intact. Joe found the matching leg and Frank added a foot.

The young people and the professor were jubilant as they arrived at camp with their prize. As the skeleton was hung up inside Thompson's tent, Nancy suddenly cocked her head. "Listen!"

In the distance, the chimes were playing!

"The ghost again!" Frank said.

"Indian ghost!" Joe added. "Say, maybe it's the ghost of this young fellow," he said, gently patting the skeleton.

Nancy had a more practical idea. "Maybe the ghost who rings the chimes is sending a message to his ghost friends. I think what we should do is go to the village tomorrow and talk to Grandma Norton, as Ben Nowall suggested."

"Good idea," Frank and Joe agreed.

The professor gave them permission to take the day off. Their plan to leave early was changed suddenly, however. At 5:00 A.M., the camp bell rang several times, summoning all the students and crew to the mess tent. Professor Thompson and four police officers stood at the head table.

When all the campers had assembled, the archeologist spoke in a heavy voice. "No one is to leave here until you have all been questioned and a thorough search has been made. During the night, our skeleton disappeared!"

"You mean it was *stolen*?" Frank called out.

"Stolen, hidden, or buried," Thompson answered. "You are to tell the police anything and everything you know about it. Don't leave here without permission."

The officers stepped forward and began their investigation. After an hour's questioning and a search of the tents and grounds, nothing had been discovered. The professor and his students were baffled and upset.

Professor Thompson announced finally, "You young people are excused. Those wishing to work at the dig may do so. There'll be a bus for those of you who want to go to town."

Nancy said to Frank and Joe, "Let's carry out our plan and call on Grandma Norton."

The bus driver knew the Norton home and stopped there to let the three detectives out. Fortunately, the smiling, white-haired woman was at home. Nancy introduced herself and the boys, then said they would like to talk about the mystery mountain and its history.

"Come right in," Mrs. Norton invited. "The mountain is dear to my heart."

Some of the information she offered had already been learned from Ben Nowall, but the rest was startling news.

"We descendants of the original settlers are being frightened and threatened by a lot of people!"

"Real people?" Nancy asked. "Or ghosts?"

"Both," Grandma Norton replied. "There's a group that calls itself the Preservation Society, headed by a Mrs. Witherspoon. They claim they want to buy our whole hill—but we won't sell."

"Why?" Frank asked.

"Well, you know about the epidemic. I

155

wouldn't sign off my property for all the gold in Fort Knox. My conscience wouldn't let me. The germs from an epidemic last forever. Why, over in Egypt, people broke into a tomb a thousand years after it was sealed. They caught the germs inside and died!"

Nancy, Frank, and Joe looked at one another. Frank asked Grandma Norton, "Do you think there's any connection between the Preservation Society and the ghost?"

"I don't know. The society seems mighty eager to get the property, and the ghost seems mighty anxious to keep everybody away."

"Have you any idea why anyone would want the property that badly?" Joe asked.

Grandma Norton answered quietly, "Yes, I do. I was only a very little girl when my family moved down here, but I once heard my father say to my mother, 'Too bad everybody had to leave such a great treasure behind.' Later, when I asked what it was, they wouldn't talk about it. Simply said, 'It's full of germs.'"

Nancy was puzzled and thoughtful, and finally asked the elderly woman her theory about the ghost. "First of all, do *you* believe in ghosts?"

"I certainly do! I've seen them many a time —especially lately." At that moment, a door on the second floor slammed shut and something heavy dropped. "There he is again," she said, not looking alarmed. "*My* ghost. I live alone, you know. Listen!"

An eerie, faraway voice moaned, "Do not sell the hillside!"

In a flash, Joe was out of his chair and bounding up the stairs. Frank followed. Nancy waited just long enough to ask if it was all right, and dashed up the steps. She wondered why Grandma Norton was so calm.

The Hardy boys were already searching the second floor for an intruder. They checked under beds, behind draperies, and in every closet. One door in the hall was locked. Nancy went to ask Mrs. Norton about it.

"That's the entrance to the back stairs. I always keep it locked, top and bottom. Never use it."

"Would you mind unlocking it now?" Nancy asked. "The ghost may be hiding there."

The woman smiled. "I'll do it to please you, but you won't find anything."

She brought the key and opened the door from the kitchen end. Nancy held her breath. The next second, the elderly woman gave a fearful shriek.

On the steps lay a long white sheet. At the top

of it was a skull. Balls of fire gleamed from the eye sockets!

The woman's cry sent Frank and Joe flying to the first floor. They found Nancy trying to calm Grandma Norton, who wailed, "Who put that horrible thing here?"

Opening the door further, the boys cautiously inspected the ghost. There was nothing under the sheet. "Mrs. Norton, who besides yourself has a key to the stairway doors?" Frank asked, completely mystified.

"Nobody," the woman replied, "but ghosts don't need keys. The one I've seen and heard always comes at night—usually outdoors—and has never touched or harmed anyone. The whole figure seems to be filmy and white."

The three detectives felt sure there was some connection between this house, the Norton home on the hillside, the chimes, and the ghost.

Frank asked the woman, "Would you let us go into your house on the hill?"

"And get the germ that killed a lot of my ancestors? No, no. I couldn't be responsible for your deaths."

Joe told her they were not afraid. "Besides, we can open all the windows. Germs don't like sunshine and fresh air!"

Grandma Norton smiled. "Well, all right, if

you're very careful. I suppose it'll be the only way to find out what's going on. I'll give you the key to the front door. But first I'll fix you some lunch."

While she was doing this, Nancy, Frank, and Joe nailed shut both doors to the stairway so the mysterious intruder could no longer use it.

During the meal, Grandma Norton was quiet, but at the end she said, "I think I can trust you young folks with a secret. My father had a box he insisted on bringing from the hill house. It was kept locked. A couple of years ago, I found the key that fit it. Inside was a letter. My father had written that he had found relics of human bones and thought the hillside had been an Indian burial ground. With the bodies there was jewelry containing precious stones."

Nancy had an idea. "Could someone else know the secret and be trying to scare people away? Then they'd have a chance to dig up the treasure."

Joe added to her theory. "Maybe the digging has already started. The chimes ringer could watch from the tower and alert friends to cover their work and hide."

"What puzzles me," Frank said, "is why we didn't see any evidence of digging."

The three young detectives hurried off, carrying the key to the Norton family homestead on the hill. How quaint the house was! It was completely furnished, and there were even logs laid in the fireplace. Outside of a few cobwebs and a layer of dust, the place was immaculate.

Frank pointed to footprints across the patterned, dusty carpet on the floor. The three sleuths started a search for an intruder or a hidden treasure, but found neither. Nancy was not ready to give up, but Frank and Joe decided to go outside and look. After finding nothing suspicious, they stopped at an old well in the backyard.

"If thieves were about to be caught with stolen goods," Frank said, "they could quickly throw them into the well!"

"They sure could," Joe agreed and inspected the bucket and rope which, though old, seemed sturdy. He straddled the bucket and asked Frank to hold the rope and let him down.

"Let 'er rip!" he called with a grin to his brother.

Pulling a flashlight from his pocket, Joe determined that the water at the bottom was shallow.

"Frank, there's something here!" He fished around in the water and examined an object with his light. Hey—it's full of relics!"

He began to pick up not only human bones but beaded necklaces, arm bands, and a turquoise headband. Excited, he scooped up everything he could, putting the small pieces into his pockets and holding the rest in his arms.

"Frank, pull me up!" he shouted, and began the ride topside.

He was almost at the top when Frank saw that part of the rope was fraying. In a moment, it might snap and Joe would go crashing to the bottom! Frank grabbed his brother's shoulders and yelled, "Get out, Joe! Quick!"

Joe nimbly caught the edge of the well and with Frank's help, hoisted himself from the bucket. The next moment the rope parted and the bucket splashed at the bottom.

"Wow! That was close!" Joe exclaimed.

"Too close," added Frank, gazing at his brother's armful of bones.

At that moment, they were startled by a cry from Nancy.

"Frank! Joe! Help!"

Frank dashed to the front door of the house and hurried inside. Joe ran around to the far side.

Both boys were in time to see a man climbing out of a window. He was holding a full-length skeleton!

"Grab him!" Nancy exclaimed. "That's our skeleton!"

With a strong boy on either side of him, the thief had no chance to get away. Nancy took the skeleton. On a leg bone were the letters TD, the identification for Thompson dig.

"I found this behind a wall panel," Nancy explained, gently placing the skeleton on the floor. "Through a knothole in the wood, I could feel a spring that opened the panel. The skeleton was hanging in there. While I was looking for an identification mark, this man came up and took the relic. I was afraid the skeleton would break if we fought over it, so I yelled for you."

Frank turned to the thief, who was struggling to get away.

"Who are you?" he demanded.

No answer. Joe said, "I'll bet you're the one who has been playing ghost around these hills."

He was about to ask if he was also the chimes player, when the bells rang out. This time, however, there was not a musical tune, but a noisy jangle. Nancy detected a fleeting but smug smile on the face of their prisoner and wondered if this was a special kind of signal.

The next moment, they were startled to see a

police car approaching. Two officers stepped out and the thief was handed over to them.

"You must be psychic," Frank said, mopping his forehead. "How did you know we needed you?"

Officer Kinton explained, "Grandma Norton had an uneasy feeling about what might be happening up here. She asked us to come and find you."

Officer Ruskin tried to interrogate the thief but he still would say nothing. Nancy took the boys aside. "Since we found one stolen relic in a house," she said, "why wouldn't the thieves use other houses to hide stolen loot?"

"Nifty deduction," said Frank.

He then told Nancy and the two officers about the relics and jewels that he and Frank had found in the well. He asked Ruskin about entering each house on the hillside to look for stolen relics.

"Under the circumstances," the officer said, "I think the owners would agree. I'll find out in town after we lock up this prisoner."

After they drove off, Nancy said, "I think we should search Grandma Norton's home one more time."

They made a thorough check but found nothing until they came to the basement. By flashlight, the detectives became aware of a suspicious mound in the earthen floor. A shovel stood in a corner. Very carefully, Frank dug out the dirt. Underneath a layer of soil lay many Indian artifacts, mostly jewelry.

Nancy, Frank, and Joe wondered if this could be part of the valuable collection Grandma Norton's father referred to in the paper she had found. Officers Kinton and Ruskin arrived shortly and were shown the latest find.

"Amazing!" said Ruskin. "You three really *are* detectives. Well, here's more work for you."

He took a box of keys from his pocket and handed it to Frank. "The townspeople are pretty excited about your theory. Perhaps other houses on the hill have loot hidden in them. I wish we could stick around to help, but I'm afraid the department is shorthanded."

Joe said, "Would it be okay if we asked Professor Thompson and the students at the dig to help us?"

"Great idea," Ruskin replied.

Frank used his walkie-talkie to call the dig, and the invitation to help solve the mystery of the cursed hill was eagerly accepted.

In the meantime, the three young sleuths inspected houses near Grandma Norton's. All of them had secret compartments in cupboards, desks, and chimneys. Some of these held articles belonging no doubt to the homeowners, but many other pieces were marked and the detectives were sure these had been hidden by the relic thieves. They were convinced of this when they came upon a shrunken skull on which was the imprint HOPEWELL MUSEUM.

"What are we going to do with all this stuff?" Joe asked. "Set up shop? How much am I bid for this fine old Indian skull? Very intelligent man—see how his skull protrudes?"

Joe's nonsense was interrupted by the arrival of Professor Thompson and his student diggers. Among them was Nancy's tentmate, Jenny Gardner. After looking around and hearing the full story, she shivered.

"This place is weird," she said. "When does the ghost come on?"

"Right now," Nancy replied, as the chimes suddenly began to sound. This time it was a pretty tune, as if played by a ghostly musician.

Joe looked at Frank. "There's that warning again. I say we give the others the keys and we three get over to that church and find the chimes player!"

After giving instructions to the newcomers, the three detectives started off. When they arrived at the church, they found that the ladder to the tower had been removed again.

"Guess we'll have to use the old ivy overhand," Frank said, flexing his muscles.

At that moment, they saw a trapdoor in the floor opening. "Nancy, hide!" Frank whispered. He motioned to Joe to stand guard on one side of the trapdoor, while he took the other. Presently, the top of a long ladder appeared, then a man. He did not notice the young people and raised the ladder to the tower opening. The stranger scampered up the rungs and disappeared.

Frank and Joe instantly removed the ladder and Joe whispered to Nancy, "One more prisoner for us!"

"I wonder what's in the basement," she said.

"Joe and I'll check that out," Frank said. "You be our lookout."

The boys beamed flashlights into the basement, then eased the ladder down. They left the trapdoor open. For some time, there was not a sound from either the tower or the basement. Then, suddenly, Nancy became aware of a commotion below and a man's angry voice, "This time you kids are going to pay for your spying. You'll drown, and nobody will ever find you here! In the meantime, we'll escape from this watery dungeon!"

Nancy waited no longer. She covered the

distance back to Grandma Norton's in record time. Quickly, she told the diggers to carry their tools and rush up to the church. "Rescue Frank and Joe from the basement. They're in great danger. And try to catch the thieves!"

Breathlessly, Nancy rushed from house to house alerting the students, who had already discovered many old Indian relics. Some bore identifying marks of museums and private collections. Professor Thompson offered to stay and guard the homes on the hillside. Nancy followed the last digger to the church, wondering with a sinking heart what might have happened to Frank and Joe.

The Hardys, securely tied, sat in a corner watching members of the relics robbery gang climb the ladder, their arms full of historic treasures. The boys struggled to free themselves, but in vain.

Before the last man left, he turned on a large faucet, letting out a heavy stream of water. He chuckled.

"Enjoy your swim, boys," he said. When he reached the top of the ladder, he pulled it up and slammed the trapdoor shut.

Outside the church, Nancy could see quite a commotion. As the thieves emerged, the diggers, armed with picks and shovels, captured them one by one.

Nancy asked frantically, "Where are Frank and Joe Hardy?"

One man sneered. "We didn't bring 'em. Let 'em drown! Serves 'em right for bein' where they shouldn't!"

The ladder lay on the floor. Quickly, it was put into the hole, and a boy named Jerry raced down. His friend Jeff followed. By now, the gushing water was up to the Hardys' chests. Their camp friends used pocket knives to release Frank and Joe, who waded over to the pipe and turned off the water. Perspiration covered their brows.

"Thanks for saving these two relics," Joe said, grasping his brother's shoulder and grinning at Jerry and Jeff.

As the Hardys and their rescuers rushed up the ladder, they heard loud arguments outside. By this time the police, summoned by Professor Thompson over his car telephone, had taken charge. The prisoners, including the man in the chimes tower, were identified by the officers as members of a worldwide group of thieves who dealt in priceless relics and sold them in foreign markets. These prisoners had concentrated on early American Indian artifacts.

After the police had sped off with them, Professor Thompson congratulated the young detectives. "I've always prided myself on being a pretty first-rate digger," he said with a grin. "But you three did some pretty fair digging yourselves!"

The young people laughed, and Nancy gazed up at the church tower. "You know," she said, "If it hadn't been for the tolling of the chimes, we might not have been led to the thieves so quickly!"

Just then, the group heard the rattling school bus coming up the hill. Instead of sightseers, it was carrying only four people: Ben Nowall, Grandma Norton, a younger woman, and a boy of fifteen. News had already reached town about the happening on the hill.

The elderly woman was overjoyed, and praised Nancy, Frank, and Joe. With an obvious blush she said, "That ghost in my house was my *grandson*, who likes to play tricks on me. He found a duplicate key to my back stairway and placed the sheet and skull with those horrible eyes to scare me. Well, he did, all right. As if those nighttime haunts weren't enough! And he told me he dug up that skull on this hillside!"

Ben walked over to the group. "You young folks are smarter'n I gave you credit for, but in a way I'm sorry you solved the mystery. Now I won't have nothin' to tell the tourists!"

The other woman and the boy now got out of the bus and were introduced as Mrs. Witherspoon, president of the Preservation Society, and her son, a musician. "We *must* keep the hillside as a special historic site. All the owners have agreed that if they wish to sell, they will give our group the first chance to make a bid."

"I'm so glad," Professor Thompson spoke up, "because I think excavations here will reveal an entire Indian culture, undiscovered as yet."

Grandma Norton smiled, then said, "We'll never forget these fine young detectives who risked their lives to bring peace and preservation to our homes. And I'm glad that the fear of the epidemic is now over."

At that moment, the chimes in the church tower rang out triumphantly.

Nancy, astonished, turned to Frank and Joe, but they were gone! Also the magician! She looked to see them smiling and waving out of the tower of the church.

THE SECRET OF MOUNTAINTOP INN

"**T**his is the worst snowstorm I've ever been in," said Karen Young to Nancy Drew, who was driving them both up the precipitous road to Mountaintop Inn.

"I'm afraid it's a real blizzard," Nancy replied. "I'll be glad when we reach the—oh!"

The car suddenly jerked out of control on the icy road. Nancy turned the wheel into the skid and barely managed to avoid a high, solid-looking snowbank. Then she carefully steered the car back onto the road.

Karen was shaking with fear. "Boy, that was close," she said, her voice trembling. "Should we pull over till the snow stops?"

Nancy was worried too, but replied, "I don't want to stop. We'd certainly get stuck. The snow's pretty deep."

"It's not just the storm that's getting to me," Karen admitted. "I guess I'm upset about my cousin Sue's disappearance. Oh, I hope nothing dreadful has happened to her!"

Nancy did not dare take a hand off the steering wheel to give her friend a comforting pat. Instead, she said, "I agree, but wait till we reach the inn and start working on the mystery. I'm sure we'll be able to find her soon."

Karen sighed. "Sue and her mother were looking forward to a lovely two-week Christmas holiday, then this had to happen. The police think she's a runaway. But Cousin Sue would *never* do that!"

Nancy asked, "Isn't Sue related to Frank and Joe Hardy?"

"Yes. They're her cousins. I believe the boys have been called to help us search for Sue." For the first time, Karen's face broke into a smile. "With three great young detectives working on it, the mystery of Sue's disappearance should be solved before Christmas gets here!"

There was no time for the girl sleuth to reply. She had reached a blind turn and was sounding her horn when a small truck careened around the corner. It was headed straight for Nancy's car!

In a flash, she had to decide whether to stay

in the truck's path or veer to the edge of the precipice, where she might not be able to stop and would surely crash down the cliff. But she had to take that chance! Quickly, she pulled over as the truck zigzagged past.

Paralyzed with fear, Karen had closed her eyes. When nothing happened, she slowly blinked at Nancy, who let out a sigh of relief at having avoided disaster. Her face was grimly determined as she pulled back onto the road and once more climbed the hill.

"Nancy, you're a wonder!" Karen exclaimed, giving her friend an affectionate kiss on the cheek.

The young detective said, "Thanks. It was touch and go for a few seconds."

Karen asked if she had seen the driver's face. "Yes," Nancy said, "but I caught only a glimpse. The man behind the wheel was angular and pinched-looking. The kind of face that could give you a nightmare."

"Then I don't want to meet him," Karen said.

"I do," Nancy disagreed. "I'd like to ask him why he was driving so recklessly."

Within five minutes, Mountaintop Inn came into view, hazy in the driving snow and gale winds. But the sturdy stone building looked very attractive, with its lighted windows filled with poinsettias and Christmas decorations. Nancy pulled under the porte-cochere and the doorman helped the girls unpack the snow-covered car.

"Glad you made it safely," he said. "Pretty bad driving."

"Yes," Nancy replied. "A man in a small truck nearly hit our car. Was he from here?"

"I guess so. This is the end of the road. What did he look like?"

After Nancy described the driver's face, the doorman said, "He's Maury Spindar, who rooms with Santa Claus." When the girls' eyebrows shot up, he explained, "I mean the gentleman who *plays* Santa Claus."

The doorman set the luggage inside the lobby. As Nancy registered at the desk, Karen hurried toward a woman standing near a huge stone fireplace in which crackling logs sent up multicolored flames.

"Aunt Janet!" she exclaimed and hugged Sue Hardy's mother. "We made it!"

"I was worried about you," said the pretty but haggard-looking woman. "Oh, I'm so glad you and Nancy are here. I'm sick over Sue's disappearance."

By this time, Nancy had walked over and after greetings asked for the latest news.

"There is none, except a rather strange clue. A child, who is no longer here, declared she saw Sue being kidnapped by Santa Claus!"

Karen stared at her aunt. "That sounds silly. The child's imagination must have been working overtime."

Nancy made no comment. As a sleuth, she knew there might be some truth, however slight, in any story connected with a mystery. She asked, "What made the child mention Santa Claus?"

Janet Hardy explained that every afternoon, when tea was served in the lounge, a man dressed as Santa Claus told stories to the children. "Then he leads everyone in the singing of Christmas carols and songs. I've attended, but I'm afraid my heart hasn't been in it." A tear trickled down Aunt Janet's cheek and her voice choked up as she added, "I just want Sue back."

Karen put an arm around her and Nancy was about to add a hopeful word when she saw two boys come into the lobby from outdoors. They had brushed an accumulation of snow from their hiking clothes and boots and shaken it out of their woolen caps.

"Frank and Joe!" Nancy exclaimed and went to greet the two Hardys. The boys in turn gave her snowy kisses.

"I'm glad you're here," Frank said. "We've chased down every clue, but no luck."

Joe added, "We've tramped the woods but found no trace of her. Maybe Santa took her to the North Pole!"

The brothers removed their heavy jackets, then Joe said, "We'll go to our room and leave this gear. Be right back. But, Nancy," Joe paused, "we did learn one thing that's very hush-hush. Valuable jewelry has been stolen from several guests, but there aren't any suspects so far and the manager wants no publicity. We wonder if the thief may be staying here."

With that, the brothers hurried off. Nancy and Karen, too, went to their room to change into comfortable indoor clothes. By the time the four young people met again on the first floor, the afternoon's entertainment had started in the large lounge.

A beautifully decorated Christmas tree had been set up and was aglow with tiny lights. Near it sat Santa Claus in a gilded armchair.

At the sound of sleigh bells, he began to tell a story to the children seated on the floor around him. It was about a little boy who dreamed that his Christmas toys came to life and performed for him. Santa was very dramatic, changing the tone of his voice for each character and imitating the sounds of the animals. The children were fascinated and applauded loudly at the end.

During the refreshment period that followed, Nancy asked one of the porters if Santa was an actor. The answer was no, he was a minister. She reported this to the Hardy boys.

Joe said, "That explodes an idea I had that Santa might have something to do with the thefts of jewelry. But not a minister!"

Frank added, "And with Sue's disappearance. By the way, Nancy, rumors are going around that she was kidnapped."

"You mean by Santa Claus?" Nancy asked with a broad grin.

"Sure," Joe answered. "He took her up the chimney in his pack!"

After laughing for a moment, Nancy and the boys joined Karen and Mrs. Hardy for refreshments and tried to cheer up the downcast woman. While Sue's mother was trying to be brave, she kept expressing her worry, together with her disappointment that the authorities were not doing anything.

With a sad smile, she said, "I'm counting on you young detectives to find my daughter."

Frank spoke up. "I'm sorry we can't do any more tonight, Aunt Janet. But first thing tomorrow we'll start out again."

Fortunately, the weather had cleared by the

following morning. The road from the inn had been plowed. When the young people met at breakfast, the Hardys wondered where they should start their search.

Nancy had a suggestion. "I have a strong hunch that Maury Spindar, who nearly hit Karen and me yesterday, was on an urgent and mysterious errand, because he drove so fast and recklessly. Would you two drive into town with me and see if we can find out where he had to go in that blinding snowstorm? Karen, do you mind?"

"Not at all. I think I should stay with Aunt Janet, anyway."

"Let's go pronto," Frank urged.

In less than an hour, the three were entering the small town of Gordon. Frank drove slowly along the main street. The young sleuths looked curiously at stores and office buildings, trying to weave possible threads into a solution. But they found nothing that looked the least bit suspicious.

They had nearly reached the end of the block when Joe cried out, "Frank! Stop a minute! There's someone who might give us a clue!" He pointed toward a restaurant with a wide, plate-glass window across the front. A cashier was seated at a desk near the door sorting order slips.

"Good idea," Nancy agreed.

Frank parked the car and the three went inside. They ordered mugs of hot chocolate and apple pizzas with crunch topping from a young waitress. While the snack was being prepared, Nancy sauntered up to the cashier's desk, which had an attached glass case containing confections and a few newspapers and magazines.

As Nancy eyed them, the woman remarked, "Those papers are two days old, honey. In that blizzard yesterday, nothing was delivered."

"Another girl and I were caught in the storm driving up to the inn," Nancy said. "A man in a truck was speeding down and nearly crashed into us. By any chance, did you see a dark-colored truck around town with a thin-faced driver?"

"As a matter of fact, I did," the woman replied. "It was snowing so hard that no one was here. I was standing at the window watching the storm when a strange man drove up. He jumped out of his truck, hurried to a car along the curb, and handed a package to a fellow inside."

Nancy asked what kind of a car it was. "A green compact," the cashier replied. "The window on the passenger side had a big crack in it."

"Where did the men go?"

"The one in the car drove off," the woman answered. "The fellow in the truck came in here and ordered coffee."

"Did he talk to you?"

"Not a word." The cashier smiled. "Between you and me, I think he was nuts. He kept mumbling to himself."

"Did you overhear anything?" Nancy inquired.

"He grumbled about the weather and mentioned something about 'dying from the cold in that Twin Brook Cabin.'"

Nancy was intrigued by the information, but tried not to show her mounting excitement. She bought a magazine, then thanked the woman and returned to their table.

Frank and Joe were already munching pizzas. "Excuse us for not waiting," Frank apologized, "but they smelled so good."

"It's okay," said Nancy. "Listen! I may have a wonderful clue to where Sue is being held!" She repeated the information.

Joe said quickly, "Sounds like a good lead. We mustn't waste any time starting a search."

The three left hurriedly after Joe paid the check. Driving as fast as he dared on the slippery mountain road, Frank finally reached the inn. Nancy suggested that they ask Karen to join them on their search for Twin Brook Cabin. She saw her friend in the lounge with Mrs. Hardy. Nancy explained the latest clue.

"Oh, I hope you find my Sue alive and unharmed!" the woman exclaimed, trembling.

Nancy put an arm around Mrs. Hardy's shoulders and gave her a little hug. "I have a very strong hunch that we're going to bring back some good news."

"I hope so."

Meanwhile, Frank Hardy went to the manager's office and asked the manager, Mr. Price, if he had ever heard of Twin Brook Cabin. Mr. Price told him that the cabin belonged to a group of men who used it during hunting season.

An ideal hiding place for a kidnapper's victim, Frank thought, but he did not mention this. Instead he asked, "Where is the place?"

"About four miles due east of here," Mr. Price replied. "After a while, you'll come to a brook. Then there's another one three hundred feet further. They merge just about where the cabin is."

Frank hurried back to his group and told them what he had learned.

"I think," Joe said, "that we should strap our

cross-country skis and poles to our backs and go to that cabin."

"In this snow," said Nancy, grinning, "mine are going on my feet!"

"I haven't any skis," Karen remarked, "but I have snowshoes. I'll take those."

Nancy agreed, then said, "In case we find Sue, she could use snowshoes too. Let's rent a pair."

Nancy rented a pair from the ski shop and took along additional thongs. Before leaving, the four trekkers stuffed their pockets with bags of dried fruits and nuts and a couple of sandwiches.

The crisp mountain air gave the group added pep as they skied through the woods.

An hour later, the trekkers reached the first brook and paused. Should they follow it down the hill or hike on to the second brook to be sure they had the right place?

Nancy suggested, "Why don't we divide forces? Two of us follow this one, the others take the next brook."

"Great!" said Joe. "Come on, Karen. Race you down the brook."

The two started off. Frank and Nancy soon reached the second brook, which took a less circuitous course, with the result that the four young sleuths met where the two streams merged.

Directly ahead stood a log cabin, half hidden by the snow banked against it.

"Look!" Nancy exclaimed. "Smoke's coming out the chimney! Somebody's inside!"

"But who?" Karen asked, her heart pounding.

The group beat a path to the door and Frank pounded on it. In a few seconds the door was opened by—Santa Claus! At least, the heavyset, beardless man wore a Santa Claus suit.

Before anyone could speak, a girl behind him rushed forward. Instantly, Karen slid out of her snowshoes and ran into the cabin.

"Sue! Sue!" she cried out. "You're alive! You're okay!" The two girls laughed and cried as they hugged each other. Then Frank and Joe bent forward to kiss their cousin.

Nancy introduced herself to Santa Claus and asked, "Are you by any chance a minister?"

"Yes, I'm the Reverend Watson."

"And you were kidnapped with Sue?"

"Yes."

"Why?"

"Come in," the clergyman said. "The people who kidnapped us won't be back."

"It all started," said the Reverend Watson,

"when Sue and I were walking along an up-stairs corridor of the inn. I still had on my Santa Claus suit after my first appearance. We saw two men come out of a bedroom, their hands loaded with jewelry that they were stuffing into their pockets. The thieves saw us and ran. We chased them down a back stairway and out-doors. Suddenly, the men stopped short and threw knockout powder in our faces. The next thing we knew we woke up here."

"Bound and cold," Sue added.

"How awful!" Karen exclaimed.

"We managed to get the ropes off and build a fire," Sue continued. "By that time, it was snowing like crazy. It turned into a blizzard. We didn't dare go out in these clothes."

"Did you have anything to eat?" Karen asked.

"A little," Sue answered. "There were some cans of food in a cupboard."

Karen, Nancy, and the Hardys were already emptying their pockets of the sandwiches and snacks they'd brought along. Sue and the rev-erend accepted them eagerly.

"We'd better start for the inn and capture those kidnappers before they skip out," Nancy urged.

Frank and Joe banked the fire, while Sue and Reverend Watson put on the boys' heavy sweaters. They found hunting boots in the cabin and lashed them to the rented snowshoes for Sue.

"My Santa Claus boots are heavy," the minister said. "I'll be okay, even without snowshoes."

By the time the group reached the inn, the afternoon entertainment was in progress. Through a window, they could see the fake Santa Claus leading the group in song.

"He's one of the kidnappers!" Sue exclaimed.

Frank suggested that she and the reverend hide in a room near the rear door of the inn, while the others made sure the thieves could not escape. Karen went directly to Aunt Janet and whispered the good news while Nancy, Frank, and Joe hurried to the manager's office.

"Mr. Price," Nancy said in a low voice, "we've solved the mystery. The Santa Claus in the lounge and his roommate are kidnappers and jewel thieves."

"What!" the man exclaimed.

"We found the two victims, Sue and Reverend Watson," Frank added. "I suggest you call the police at once."

"And guard all the exits from the inn," Joe added.

"And commandeer Spindar's truck," Nancy

advised. "We're sure they're the jewel thieves." She also gave the clue of their pal with the broken car window.

The manager was speechless but finally a-greed to call the police on both counts. He picked up the phone and gave several orders to his staff. When he finished, he said to the young sleuths, "I found a note on my desk, signed by the Reverend Watson, saying he had been called home suddenly and could no longer play the part of Santa Claus. Soon afterward, Spindar and his roommate, King, came in, saying they had heard about Watson leaving. King was an out-of-work actor and wanted the job. Since I didn't wish to disappoint the children, I told him yes."

"That note was a forgery," Nancy declared.

Price went on, "Just then word came of Sue Hardy's disappearance and I forgot about Santa Claus. My thanks to you fine detectives for clearing up the mystery. But I beg you to keep it quiet. We'll switch Santa Clauses, and the kidnappers can be arrested and taken away without the guests knowing what happened."

Nancy said, "How about keeping King's Santa Claus outfit? The Reverend Watson's is ruined."

Mr. Price agreed. The kidnapper-thieves, unaware of what was happening, were cornered in their room. Some of the stolen jewelry was found in the suspects' luggage. And their pal with the broken car window was captured the same day with more of the loot. The rest was recovered from pawnshops through tickets in his wallet.

The following afternoon, Nancy, Frank, Joe, and their friends gathered in the lounge to listen to the Reverend Watson and join in the singing of carols. Sue and her mother sat with their arms around each other.

Nancy, smiling, looked at the group and said, "A Merry, Merry Christmas to you all!"

THE HARDY BOYS® SERIES
by Franklin W. Dixon

Night of the Werewolf (#59)
Mystery of the Samurai Sword (#60)
The Pentagon Spy (#61)
The Apeman's Secret (#62)
The Mummy Case (#63)
Mystery of Smugglers Cove (#64)
The Stone Idol (#65)
The Vanishing Thieves (#66)
The Outlaw's Silver (#67)
The Submarine Caper (#68)
The Four-Headed Dragon (#69)
The Infinity Clue (#70)

You will also enjoy

THE TOM SWIFT® SERIES
by Victor Appleton

The City in the Stars (#1)
Terror on the Moons of Jupiter (#2)
The Alien Probe (#3)
The War in Outer Space (#4)
The Astral Fortress (#5)
The Rescue Mission (#6)

NANCY DREW MYSTERY STORIES®
by Carolyn Keene

You will also enjoy
THE LINDA CRAIG™ SERIES
by Ann Sheldon